# MY ANGELS, MY DEVILS

## a debacle of epic proportions

My Angels, My Devils:
a debacle of epic proportions

Published by
GüRider Press

Printed in the United States of America
Cover art by Michael Turchin
Book design by Matthew Lampert

My Angels, My Devils:
a debacle of epic proportions

..............................

the selected poems, short stories and ramblings of

# Ryan Fox

GüRider Press • Los Angeles

No one escapes LA... not even the mammoths.

## tug of war

silly as it may seem
you get rope-burn
on your hands
holding onto a dream
but
silly as it may sound
your hands
will hurt worse
if you set it down

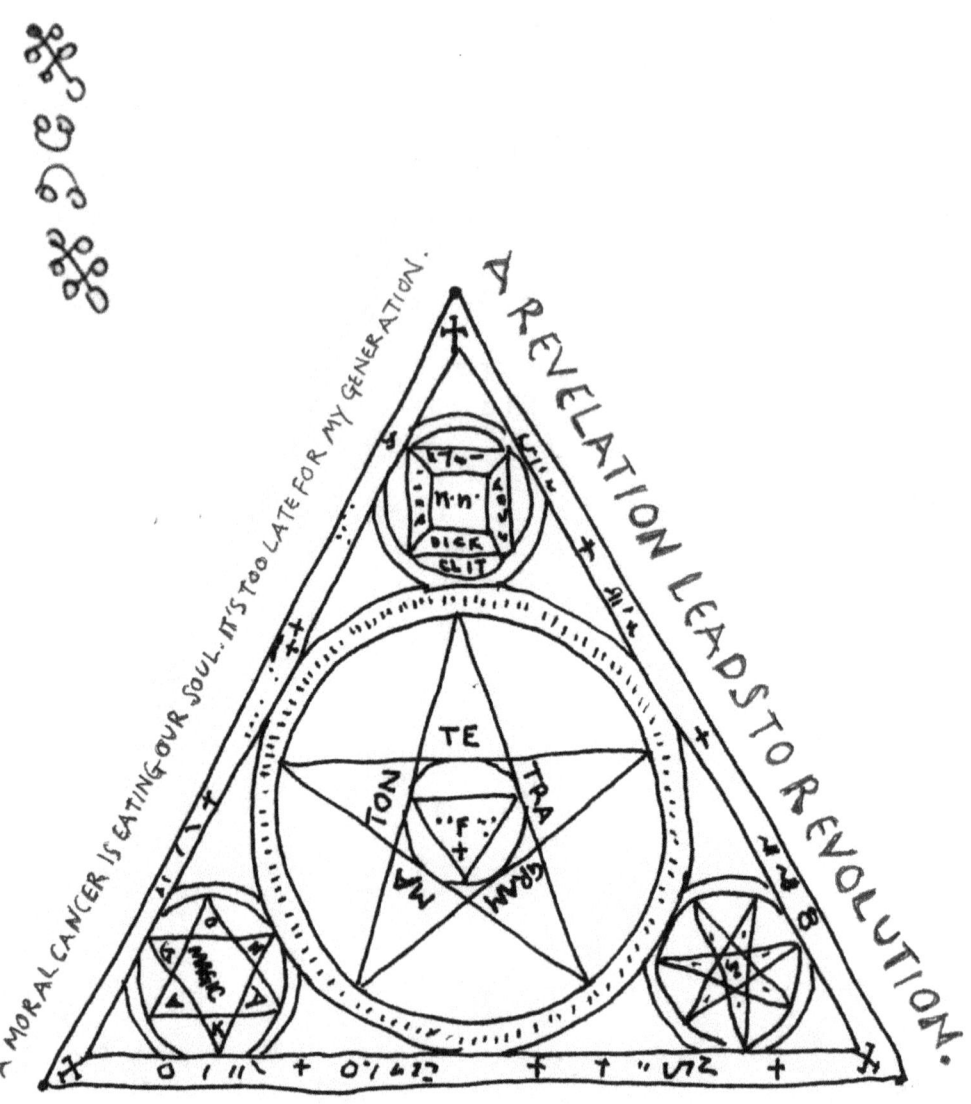

A REVELATION LEADS TO REVOLUTION.

A MORAL CANCER IS EATING OUR SOUL. IT'S TOO LATE FOR MY GENERATION.

I CAN PINPOINT THE EXACT MOMENT OF MY EVOLUTION, SITTING INSIDE
A DARK MOVIE THEATER, I BEGAN TO QUESTION "WHY".

**bamboozled**

searching for peace
in an america i never found
at night
went to sleep
the next day awoke
and was famous
mainstream
part of the commercial-machine
therefore catering to the consumer
they thought it inventive
then labeled me a beatnik
plastered my image across magazine covers
force-fed comparisons to what
"On the Road" did for Kerouac's generation
critics attacked my work
objected to the way i wrote
revolutionary
radical and sensual
figured there's nothing new in that
slowly became mocked by the mainstream
then absorbed by it
every late-night
chain-smoking
talk show guest appearance
reformed a cult following
then life ended
was nothing more than a pop culture-reference
on a tv sitcom
a trivial pursuit question

## exit row located

looking down from a plane
everything's the same
my thoughts are no different than yours
gaseous airplane food plays no favorites here
lasagna with a non-meat sauce
or fresh roasted chicken
take a guess
make a choice
be a victim
both come with salad and a sugar cookie
but on the other side of aluminum
a more appetizing infinite horizon
the earth's canvas
blotched in hues of green and brown
that subtly blend
into powder blue skies
life seems non-existent
cumulous clouds pass by
out that window
it all seems so peaceful
until the engine's hum reminding me
that the slightest mechanical glitch
can send this metal bird
plummeting towards ground zero
within a glance
all of a sudden it didn't seem too serene
begin to check the safety instruction card
all of a sudden i'm eyeballing Abdul two seats over

**i don't like to get my hair wet**

inevitably they always want
to take a shower with me afterwards
to which i usually refuse
they're sticky
from the chocolate syrup
poured on their tits
or my cum on their stomach
then it's always the same thing
whether it's three a.m. or twelve noon
i tell them where the clean towels are
then roll over in bed
cover my head with a pillow
but sometimes
if they bitch long enough
i give in and join them
the lucky ones
the ones that actually get me into the shower
think that it might lead
to us fucking again
but we don't
i just shampoo their hair from behind
kiss the nape of their neck
while telling them to finish up
i get out and towel off
go back to bed
whether its three a.m. or twelve noon

I had a dream last night that i was back in high school. One of my best friends was getting married to the singer of Coldplay. Jealous as hell, i ended up fucking one of her bridesmaids. The next thing i knew, before even having a chance to cum, i was in an enormous library with books stacked from the floor to the ceiling. It seems i had climbed to the top of a huge ladder, then began searching frantically though dirty magazines and ripping out pages to steal. Just out of reach, a coffee table book by Robert Mapplethorpe sent me tumbling towards a black hole below. Somehow i landed on my feet and suddenly was an undercover cop in the middle of a shoot out in a grimy hotel basement. At one point after ducking behind a furnace for cover, our guns turned out to be syringes and we were injecting the bad guys with AIDS. My partner got hit and we had to quickly find an antidote. Promising to check in on his family if he dies, i woke up just as i was injecting it into his leg. Go figure.

SHE READ MY POETRY AND COMPARED IT TO THE GREAT ONE. ONLY THEN, I DIDN'T KNOW WHO THE GREAT ONE WAS. STRATEGICALLY I HAD LEFT IT OUT WHILE I SHOWERED TO IMPRESS HER. I WAS DISAPPOINTED WHEN SHE DIDN'T FIND MY STYLE UNIQUE.

## THE PIED PIPER

WITH COCAINE IN YOUR POCKET
YOU'RE A GOD AMONGST MEN
THEY HANG
ON YOUR EVERY WORD
LAUGH
AT ALL YOUR JOKES
WOMEN THROW THEMSELVES AT YOU

...AND WHEN IT RUNS OUT
THEY ALL USUALLY GO HOME.

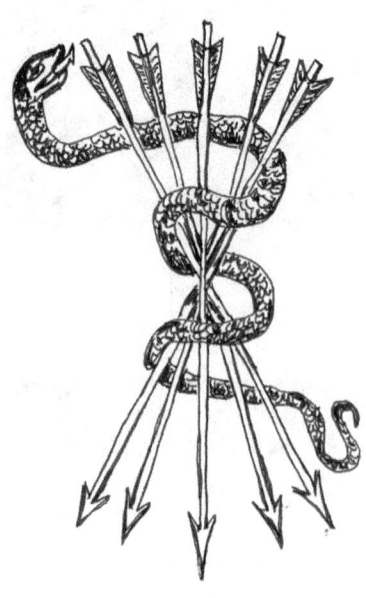

**the island of misfit toys**

most people
are like toys
shiny and plastic
boxed in attractive
colorful packaging
that lure you towards
an impulse buy
but it's only once they are
off the shelf
purchased
taken home to play with
do you discover
some pieces are missing
that they have
immovable parts
no directions
or were very poorly constructed
this is why you'll find me
on the isle
carefully examining the merchandise
then quickly putting everything back
into its box
as i found it
returning them onto the shelf
for some other
sucker
to waste their money on
get home
then realize they
lost the receipt

**hollywood haiku**

the hollywood scene
our paths crossing on circuits
no acts need exist

## chateau tupac

Tupac Shakur found it difficult to afford three mistresses while living in the south of France. Funds eventually dry up no matter how many posthumous recordings that are released. It was because of this, that deeper and deeper Pac sank into depression. Regretting the decision to fake his own death and the day his mother, Afeni Shakur, took control of his $100-million-grossing musical estate after suing Death Row Records for royalties. On the first of each month, Afeni would wire her son's surreptitious allowance overseas into a secret Swiss bank account. This barely kept a roof over Pac's head, his belly full of baguettes, three Versace shirts in his closet, with enough left over for two French hookers and an eight-ball. On the rainy nights when depression reached its peak, Tupac would seek anonymous sanctuary in AOL online chat rooms under the screename GrandmasVagina. He deeply enjoyed the anonymity of surfing the inter-web and by chance one night, Tupac met his first "true" friend. At first the relationship was nothing more than a very casual

exchange of instant messages. But quickly escalated after Tupac asked FuddyDuddy for a photo in exchanged for a rhyme that he'd wrote. That's how the friendship of Tupac Shakur and Bob Hope came to be. In the following years, Bob Hope would make numerous trips to the south of France, in which to kick it with his homey. One night at Chateau Tupac over several bottles of wine, Bob Hope confessed while in a drunken stupor that the two shared a uniquely special bond. He said, "Yo Pac, this nigga knows exactly where you're coming from. I feel you. Motherfuckers been slippin' for years thinking my honky-ass dead too. That shit's fucked up!" Tupac always enjoyed Bob Hope's company because he kept it real. After staying up for three days in-a-row on some fish-scale sniff that Mr. Hope was able to smuggle overseas in his colonoscopy bag, the two would stumble into the town square high and drunk. Usually only functioning on a few hours of sleep, they would stand on the steps of the town mosque, arguing and fighting in French. Bob Hope had picked up the language while working his many years with the U.S.O., but Tupac couldn't speak French. He would just pretend when he was drunk and zooted out of his mind on cocaine. Very few people realize that Tupac Shakur was a classically trained actor, who had performed Shakespeare and Chekhov while attending the Baltimore School of the Performing Arts. So don't be too quick in thinking that faking your own death is a lot harder than faking a French accent.

THE NEWS CAN EASILY BE POSITIVE
THEY CHOOSE FOR IT NOT TO BE
WANT YOU TO THINK
THE WORLD'S A FUCKED UP PLACE
AND YOU HAVE NO FUTURE
SO THE SYSTEM
CAN KEEP YOU IN PLACE
WHILE ITS AFFLUENZA RUNS WILD

**digressing**

why is it so hard
to let that person go
when you've been with them
for six weeks
and fucking their brains out
for five
but alas the sex wears off
the blowjobs dry
and i'm getting comfortable
which to most isn't bad
but
i just can't see taking it
any further
i never see a future
no matter who
so ladies
please
don't take it personally
while reading this
if you've seen my cock before
love is fleeting

## product placement

you might think
life is cheap
but really
it's these damn
accessories
that kill you
designer clothes
designer drugs
consume these images
that surround you
count the billboards
on sunset boulevard
then count your blessings
not your troubles
you'll be so far out
that you'll fit right in

WE WERE
AT A BAR
JUST LIKE
THIS. I WAS
SCRIBBLING
BULLSHIT
ON NAPKINS
JUST LIKE
THESE.

INT. HIGH-RISE BUILDING - APARTMENT 3F - DAY

NICHOLAS and TOMMY, both twelve years old, enter.

After locking the front door behind them, NICHOLAS tucks
his set of latch keys attached to a shoe string around
his neck, back into his "Queens of the Stone Age" tour
shirt.

Both boys remove their backpacks and toss them onto the
dining room table.

TOMMY walks over to the 4K television, turning it on. He
then pops "G.T.A. 5" into the PlayStation 4, picks up the
controller and sits down on the plush sofa.

NICHOLAS has walked over to the freezer, removing two
packages of popsicles. Next, he opens a sugar jar,
removing a bag of extremely green marijuana before
joining TOMMY on the sofa.

While TOMMY intensely plays "G.T.A. 5", NICHOLAS begins
to roll up a joint. When finished, NICHOLAS lites it,
takes a big puff, then passes to TOMMY.

                                        FADE TO:


INT. HIGH-RISE BUILDING - APARTMENT 3F - 15 MINUTES LATER

Having finished the joint, both boys sit eating the
popsicles, playing video games and listening to the
latest "50 Cent" record.

NICHOLAS has already finished his first popsicle and is
about to move on to the second one. Before doing so, He
looks down at the finished popsicle stick.

TOMMY is now reading "Maxim" magazine.

                    NICHOLAS
          "Why did the boy stick a hose in
          his friend's ear?"

                    TOMMY
          Huh?

                    NICHOLAS
          Why did the boy stick a fucking
          hose in his motherfucking friend's
          ear?

                    TOMMY
          I don't know. Why?


                                        (CONTINUED)

CONTINUED:

                         NICHOLAS
            Because, "He wanted to brainwash
            him."

Tommy blankly stares back.

                         TOMMY
            Dude, that is the fucking
            stupidest joke I've ever heard.
            Why would they print that? I mean,
            what's the fucking point of
            putting jokes on the popsicle
            sticks if they're going to be that
            bad.

NICHOLAS doesn't respond.

                         TOMMY (CONT'D)
            Wait! I got one better than
            that... The teacher asked Jimmy,
            "Why is your cat at school today
            Jimmy?"

NICHOLAS continues to zone out.

                         TOMMY (CONT'D)
            Jimmy replied crying, "Because I
            heard my daddy tell my mommy, 'I
            am going to eat that pussy once
            Jimmy leaves for school today!'"

TOMMY cracks himself up, but NICHOLAS still hasn't
changed his expression.

                         NICHOLAS
            Dude. Popsicles are for little
            kids. They market those jokes to
            children, asshole!

                         TOMMY
            Oh yeah. Well, no... No, I guess
            they couldn't use that joke then.

                                        FADE OUT:

I WAS NUMBER ONE IN HER BOX OFFICE TWO WEEKENDS IN A ROW...
THEN A NEW THEATER OPENED UP FOR ME.

THE 4 F'S

FIND 'EM
FEEL 'EM
FUCK 'EM
FORGET 'EM

I ADMIRE PIMPS. THEY'RE GOOD BUSINESS MEN. THEY CAN TEACH A SQUARE MAN HOW TO TURN A HOE OUT.

"IF YOU'RE IN THIS GAME, YOU'VE GOT TO BE TRUE TO IT. IF YOU'RE TRUE TO IT, THIS GAME GONNA PAY OFF." - DON "MAGIC" JUAN

## la woman

people pretend to be nice
in a town
where image is everything
substance
is few and far between
shooting stars lose their luster
and crash towards the earth
just our luck
they all crash here
fairy dust in their eyes
coke up their nose
art is all marketing and sales
sunshine days and pɹɐpuɐʇs nights
undressing
your wallet with her eyes
she asks
what kind of business you're in
making sure
you're worthy of support
because
she's marrying for the money
but if you can make her
fall in love with you
all the better

**leta**

she's looking at me
or is it the exit sign above my head
turn away
make casual conversation
turn back
she's still there
watching
but can i muster up the courage
to walk across the room
doubt it
she probably has a boyfriend anyway
or at least she should
been staring into those eyes for hours
and thinking way too much into it
just introduce yourself
say hello
compliment her style
something
nervous energy increasing
looking up from my liquor
i become painfully aware of her approach
quit scribbling this shit
on that napkin
put the pen down
play it smooth
"want a drink?", she asks
while looking down into my glass of ice cubes
but before i can muster up the words
she walks back to the bar
i instinctually pick up my pen
step back into my daydreams
about the sound of her laughter
the sun upon her face
the smell of her long dark hair
in the morning
then looking up from my ice cubes
i become painfully aware of her approach
returning with a drink
i try to strike a smile similar to james dean
"put it on your tab?", she asks
before seductively sliding away
i can only nod in agreement
my eyes were too focused on her
plastic name tag

**glorifying gutter mentality**

if we glorify the gutter
then who do we have to blame
i went to sleep one night
and america
became one giant strip club
marketing sexuality
i went to sleep one night
and america
became a fishbowl existence
marketing voyeurism
i went to sleep one night
and america
became a licensed physician
marketing addiction
i went to sleep one night
and war
had nothing to do with freedom
**New World Order**
if we glorify the gutter
then who do we have to blame
i went to sleep one night
and when i awoke
america became my worst nightmare

# CHAPTER TWO

It was somewhere around three in the morning. Franklin sat back in the driver's seat and stared for several minutes at his reflection in the rearview mirror. His car, a 1968 Camaro SS the color of rotten eggs, dripped power steering fluid onto the asphalt of the grocery store parking lot.

It was something he had meant to take care of, but hadn't gotten around to it yet. Money was tight, plus it was hard to find a mechanic that worked nights.

Insomnia, which Franklin now battled for the past few months, lead him to rearrange his life and better organize his time. Taking care of errands at night would replace the long hours spent watching sensationalized twenty-four hour news.

Before leaving home, Franklin would scratch down the grocery list, gather the mail, and this night in a rush almost forgot his Marlboro jean jacket. One of his favorite possessions, it had taken a lot of hard work, dedication, plus countless cartons of cigarettes to collect enough points to purchase such a fine jacket. Dr. Robert Moose, Franklin's cardiologist, would vouch for the effort. Only after finding a spot on his left lung and later the pituitary tumor pressed against his optic nerve.

Only staring for several minutes at a time into his car's rearview mirror would stop the headaches. And this night upon doing so, Franklin was able to grasp the true meaning of life.

Unimpressed, he didn't bother to lock the car door before wandering towards the grocery store. Franklin often had these clairvoyant moments, something Dr. Moose attributed to the medication that he was on.

Once inside the store, Franklin gingerly unhinged a shopping cart. He took one of the store's advertisement papers, and started leafing through while cruising up-and-down the aisles. Upon reaching page four, in the middle of aisle three, he noticed that dog food was on sale two for one. Even though he didn't own a dog, it was pleasing to find that the feeding of one was affordable.

Over the past few months Franklin had discovered something magical about the experience of shopping during the early hours of the morning. When the first shift of workers have already lined the aisles in a labyrinth of food pallets to be stocked onto the shelves. If timed just right, you had first choice of the freshest foods. Sometimes the soy milk wouldn't expire for a month if you shopped during the right hour.

But shopping at this hour also had its downsides. The deli counter was never open, so freshly sliced meats and cheeses were unable to be purchased. This didn't bother Franklin much. He was repulsed with the notion of eating flesh or mold. Besides the smoking of five packs of cigarettes a day and the insomnia thing,

Franklin lived the very healthy life of a vegan.

With his shopping list complete, Franklin was rounding the corner when he caught sight of Leta and quickly ducked back behind the end cap of quilted toilet paper. A migraine seemed to be coming on fast as Franklin rubbed his temples in a desperate attempt to formulate some kind of way out of the current situation.

Trembling, he couldn't bear an interaction with her. Not like this. He had rehearsed over-and-over many times in his head how their first introduction would play out... and this was definitely not it. It just didn't make sense. His headache was getting worse. His soy milk was getting warm. His car was unlocked in the parking lot. His sole infatuation was checking out at the only open register.

Desperately Franklin searched the Marlboro jacket for his prescription of oxy-contin, downing the pills with a juice box he grabbed off the shelf, then put back.

Leta's yoga-toned body was the epitome of every man's dreams, and with no end in sight for his insomnia, this may be the closest to dreaming Franklin could get for months. With nervous energy increasing and his heart pounding, now was as good of a time as ever to make an approach.

The droning wheels of the cart came to an abrupt halt a few feet from the register. Franklin took a deep breath. Evaporating all fears, he pushed the shopping cart directly behind Leta in line.

Infatuated with her supple breasts, long flowing dark hair and olive skin tone, like watching a car accident, Franklin was scared to look yet he couldn't look away.

Leta didn't notice his stares. In fact she didn't even notice at all, the whole time Franklin undressing her from behind with his eyes.

Behind the register, a plump Mexican woman in her forties did however take notice then awkwardly asked Leta if she was a "discount member". To which she replied, "No". As this took place, Franklin pretended to be interested in the rack of candy and assorted flavors of bubblegum. Even though he didn't like sweets very much.

It was the first beep of Leta's three items: a cucumber, a bottle of whisky and a home pregnancy test that drew his attention back to the register. Franklin rubbed his eyes, then struggled to catch his breath as if the wind had been knocked out of him. Eventually he was able to shake it off and begin to unload his cart when suddenly...

Franklin yawned.

He didn't remember much after that point, but Franklin awoke fourteen hours later in the back seat of his car. The groceries had spoiled.

EVANGELIST
DORMITORY
DESPERATION
ELEVEN PLUS TWO
SLOT MACHINES
MOTHER-IN-LAW
PRESIDENT CLINTON OF THE USA
SNOOZE ALARMS

EVIL'S AGENT
DIRTY ROOM
A ROPE ENDS IT
TWELVE PLUS ONE
CASH LOST IN ME
WOMAN HITLER
TO COPULATE HE FINDS INTERNS
ALAS NO MORE Z'S

**don't front**

the dress matches
the heels
the heels match
the purse
and given the opportunity
i bet the bra matches the g-string
so please
don't front
mojito in your left hand
parliament light in your right
we both know
you didn't get all dressed up
on this rainy wednesday night
just to have a drink
with your girlfriend
because she was there
when you bought that dress
she knows
you've already worn it
twice
so who
are you trying to impress
must be me
over here
across the bar
the one you keep looking at
so please
don't front

**driving down sunset boulevard**

take back your images
take them all back
or i'll be forced
to rip my eyes out
sew them shut
it seems to be
the only escape
in this new decade
of bombardment
branded by wireless
brainwashed by slick editing
please take it all back
i've had my fill
a culture obsessed
with icons

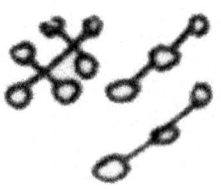

**warhol & me**

it was a great time to live
and a great time to die
a cultural storm
swept through the millennium
and at its center sat
two bemused young artists
that knew everybody
and everybody knew them
rising and fading stars
always on display
in their presence
social history written down
in ultra-sharp focus
from the corner of the room
about the paintings
the movies
the fashion
the music
if i'd gone ahead and died
ten years ago
i'd probably be a cult figure today
he always said
by recycling work
recycling people
it's very economical
running your business
as a by-product
of other businesses
a new look
a new idea
a new pair of underwear
a dark cloud forms overhead
is it raining?
he asks
no, i think they're spitting at us
hysterically we both laugh
our 15 minutes are up

## powerful words
{in order}

cancer

~~██████~~

pregnant

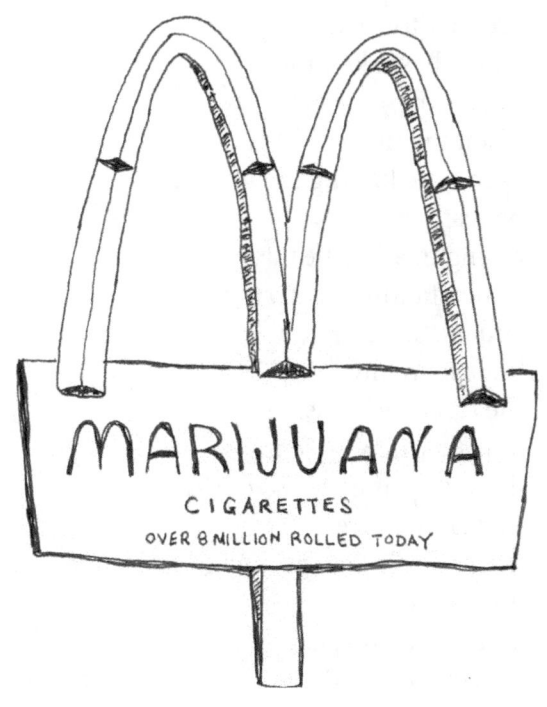

**slave to the pipe**

Sometimes in life, one must check oneself before one wrecks oneself. That's why I quit smoking weed three years ago today. That shit was controlling my life. For real. I was smoking weed first thing in the morning when I woke up. I was smoking weed last thing at night before I went to sleep. I'd smoke weed before I ate. I'd smoke weed while stuck in traffic. I'd smoke weed before I worked, played video games, listened to music or watched movies. I'd even actually smoke weed before jerking off. Basically I just had to smoke weed everyday to be able to fucking deal with people. Smoking. Smoking. Smoking. Smoking weed all fucking day long. Since I was twelve. Until one day it hit me like a ton of bricks. I realized that if I'm ever going to make this shit happen. That if I'm ever going to create a truly successful legacy in this lifetime. I have to quit smoking all this damn weed! So like I said, I'm three years clean now. All this hard work and focus is starting to pay off... and fucking finally I'll be able to start smoking weed again.

## unchained love

i set out for discovery
which has taken me
to far off
distant realms
each time kissing the ground
beneath my feet
taking in all its beauty
understanding its terrain
and customs
but eventually
the discoverer inside
longs for new adventures
discovery of uncharted isles
unchained love
then as quick as the anchor is dropped
it is raised
and set adrift again
moving forward
with the last conquest still fresh
but fading
the excitement of new
replaces the comfort of old
i've sailed many seas
in my old age
and in all of my discoveries
in all my ignorances of youth
i sailed right past
her
a place i could have called
home

We're nothing but a bunch of scared little boys, pretending to be men. Running around with our dicks in our hands trying to fuck the world. At my age,

my grandfather was half way toward his pension. I'm half way through a joint and Grand Theft Auto five. Notice i didn't say father. Because we are a generation raised by women. Even if you knew your father and he hadn't left, then he probably never was around. Or is it because we have no sense of purpose? No cause. Nothing to fight for. Well, besides oil, or rain forest or endangered species. Why can't at birth, instead of circumcision, why can't there be surgery to remove our brain from our cocks and place it back into our heads where it belongs?

**d.a.y.**

i woke up, rolled over
and before i opened my eyes
she was gone
so i just laid there
cradling the wet spot
left behind on the sheets
burying my face
deep into the pillow
where perfume and cigarettes
lingered
still lost in those green eyes
but scared of falling in love
i got up, brushed my teeth
and started another day
without her

**after 35 you have better odds being attacked by terrorists**

it doesn't take long to realize
that you've been dating
the same guy
over and over
and over again
only his name has changed
then the appetizers come
and you remember
that you always get
this first dinner date out of him
before he starts
having plans
wanting you to just
come by
his place
late night
by text message
the noncommittal
trying to keep his options open
in a world
where everything was created
in an attempt
to get laid
and some guys are good
they can stretch this shit out
for months
you think you're going
somewhere
but you're going
nowhere
fast
but he's kinda cute
and you're kinda lonely
and his car is kinda nice
so it doesn't matter
you didn't get your bikini waxed for nothing
struggling for conversation
looking for depth
while he's looking across the room
at fake tits
then the meal comes
and of course
your fettuccine alfredo has a hair in it

GOING OUT ON A DATE IS LIKE A JOB INTERVIEW, IT'S ALMOST AS IF....

PERSON #1- "I ENJOY {FILL IN THE BLANK}."
PERSON #2- "OH, I ENJOY {FILL IN THE BLANK} TOO."
PERSON #1- "NO WAY!"
PERSON #2- "OKAY, WE CAN FUCK NOW."

## this time around

i hope he's not like me
this time
you deserve better
not a single bit like me
this time
you deserve noble
because men like me
will break your heart
and wear you down
until they fracture

   your will


      your womb


         your welfare

caught up in themselves
so please
this time around
dream of qualities
scribble them down in your heart
and don't settle
because men like me
will come and go
for the rest of your life
so please
don't settle
i hope he's not like me
this time
you deserve special

$$$$$$$$$$$$

if money
wasn't tied
to love
i'd be a billionaire by now
add it all up
all the dinners
and the movies
the coffee
and the drinks
with all the random women
that went nowhere fast
and what do you get?
well
maybe i wouldn't fuck so good
but i'd be rich enough
to pay for lessons

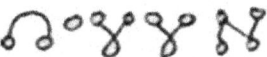

**orifice**

you were just a hole
in which to burry
my cock
and don't take that
as a compliment
because i also stick
it
in socks and cantaloupes
to get off

## guilt by association

even behind rose colored glasses
true colors shine through
                    so watch your back
          watch your words
information is always misconstrued
acquaintances
will pat a knife into your back
while telling the whole world
that the two of you
have history
future friendships sometimes hinge
on back alley bar gossip
                    so watch your back
          watch your words
watch who has something to gain
from your demise
social climbing, get it
they need to step on you

**i got a broken toilet seat**

she's scared to take a piss
afraid she might fall off
hit her head
which by the way
she already did
but drunk
so soon i guess
i'll have to get around
to fixing it
hell
she doesn't go through
my drawers
check my cell
or open
my medicine cabinet
it's good like that
when she exited
she remarked
"sounds like there's pigeons outside."
i wrote it down

**love**

let me love you
all night baby
before you fall asleep
in my arms
let me wake you with kisses
in the morning baby
before you have to get up
i've never felt this way before
i don't think you quite much understand
that i taught myself to be this man
and i'm still learning
but right now
i know enough
to make you laugh
enough
to make you happy
enough
to turn you onto
your stomach
arch your hips into
your favorite position
slowly remove your underwear
then press
the warm wet cotton against my face
instantly infatuated
i could eat every last inch of you
drink ever last drop
you have to offer

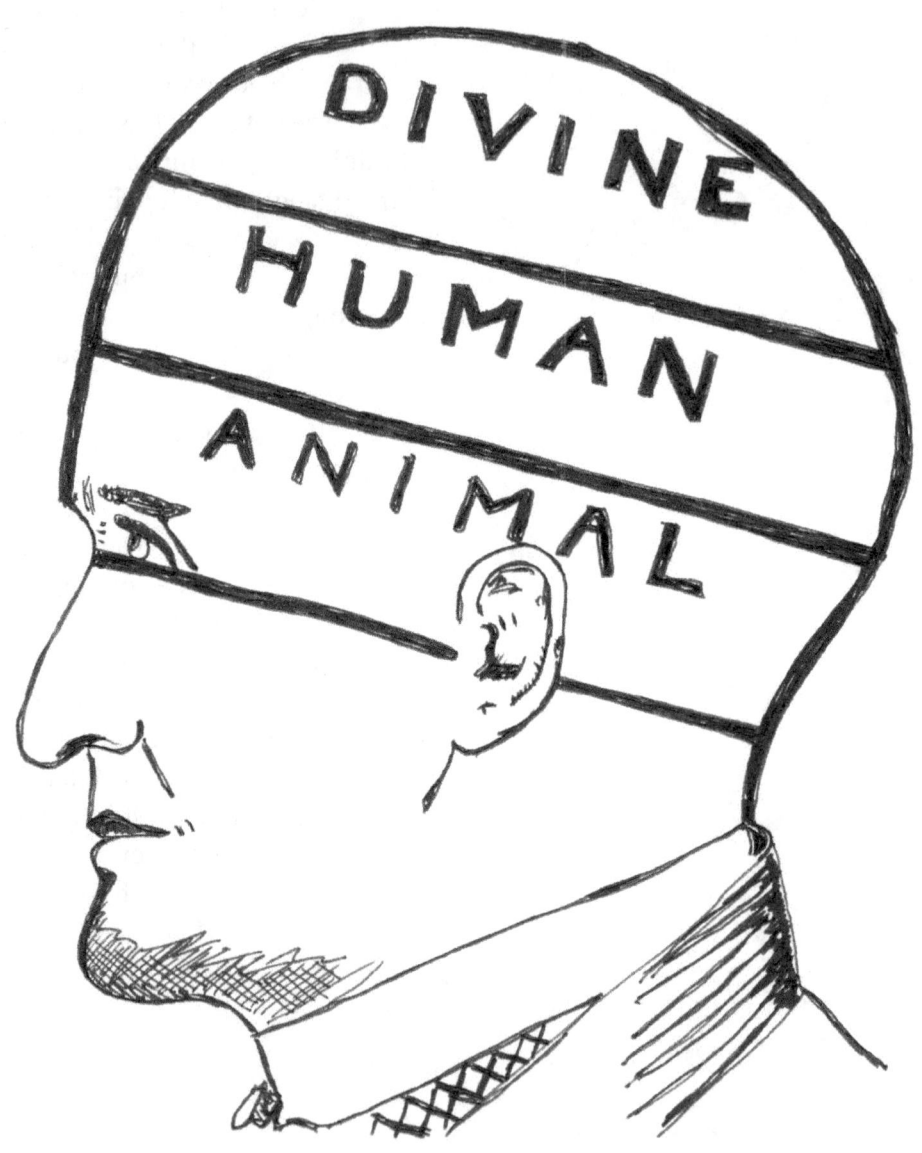

# Map of Consciousness

[Robin Williams]

### jimmy christ

jesus's brother
was named jim
a plumber
not a carpenter
and when they went
to the beach
as children
jesus would walk
on water
and heal people
jim
would just get
sand up his ass

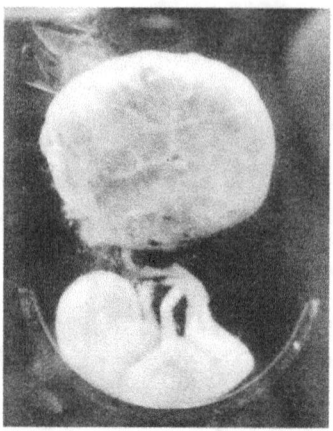

## vocation pro quietus

I'm not saying that I'd like to work there for the rest of my life, but abortion clinics have always fascinated me. Haven't you ever wanted to step in-between the stirrups and suck out someone's unwanted love? Moments before entering the examination room, you'd pause at the door, listening to the couple's conversation. After peeing into a pregnancy test and seeing a "+" sign she'd say...

*"Fuck. How could this have happened? I've been on the pill since I was fifteen."*

The father, strangely quiet at first, would later explain that he was wondering if he was still on the guest list that night at Sky Bar. After regaining his train of thought he'd say to her...

*"How do I even know it's mine?"*

Which is naturally upsetting and leads her to say that she...

*"Never has one-night stands!"*

But he interjects,...

*"Yeah right! You fucking did it with me, you probably do it with everybody! You whore."*

It's around this time that she slaps him. Then he says...

*"Fuck this shit!"*

He leaves the examination room and bumps into you at the door. This would be the first time that you actually got a good look at him and notice his nationality. After realizing he's half-black, half-chinese, the first thought that might cross your mind might be...

*"If he stole a car, would he be able to drive it?"*

Not that I'm racist, my father's half-drunk. Eventually when he's cooled off in the waiting room, he'll return out of some sort of obligation to do the right thing. By this time. Hopefully. You have your hand inside. Somewhere around her uterus.

WORDS ARE the
CHANCE WE TAKE
BUT WAS it Better
 leFt unexplained.

Made from 100% recycled fiber,
containing 30% post-consumer material.

He LooKED BUT
She WAS NoweRe to
 Be FouND.

He Hoped She'd Soon
FoRGet everything
tHAt He'd SHARed.

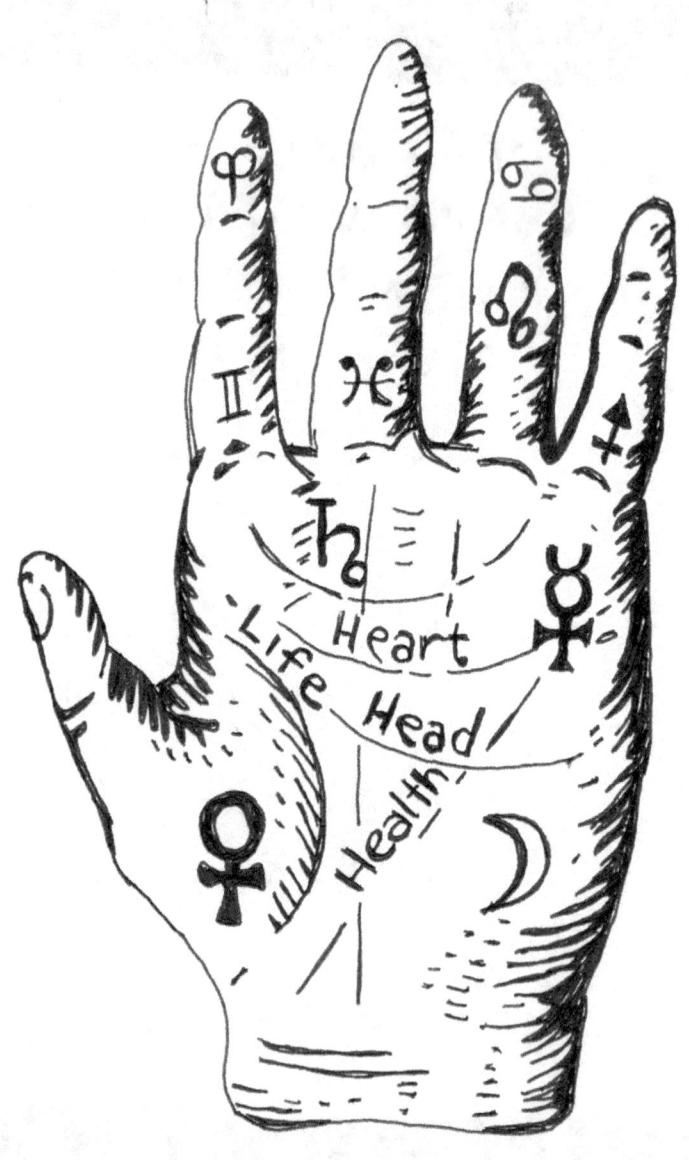

I HAVE INTRICATE SYSTEMS WITH WOMEN.

**my swisher sweet**

you only call
when you want something
and mostly it's for me
to come over
smoke a blunt
and have
meaningless sex
attracted to my
        intense conversation
oral fixation
        and deep penetration
but really
what turns you on
is only the
deeper complications
between us

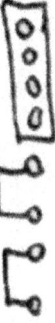

BRITNEY SWALLOWS

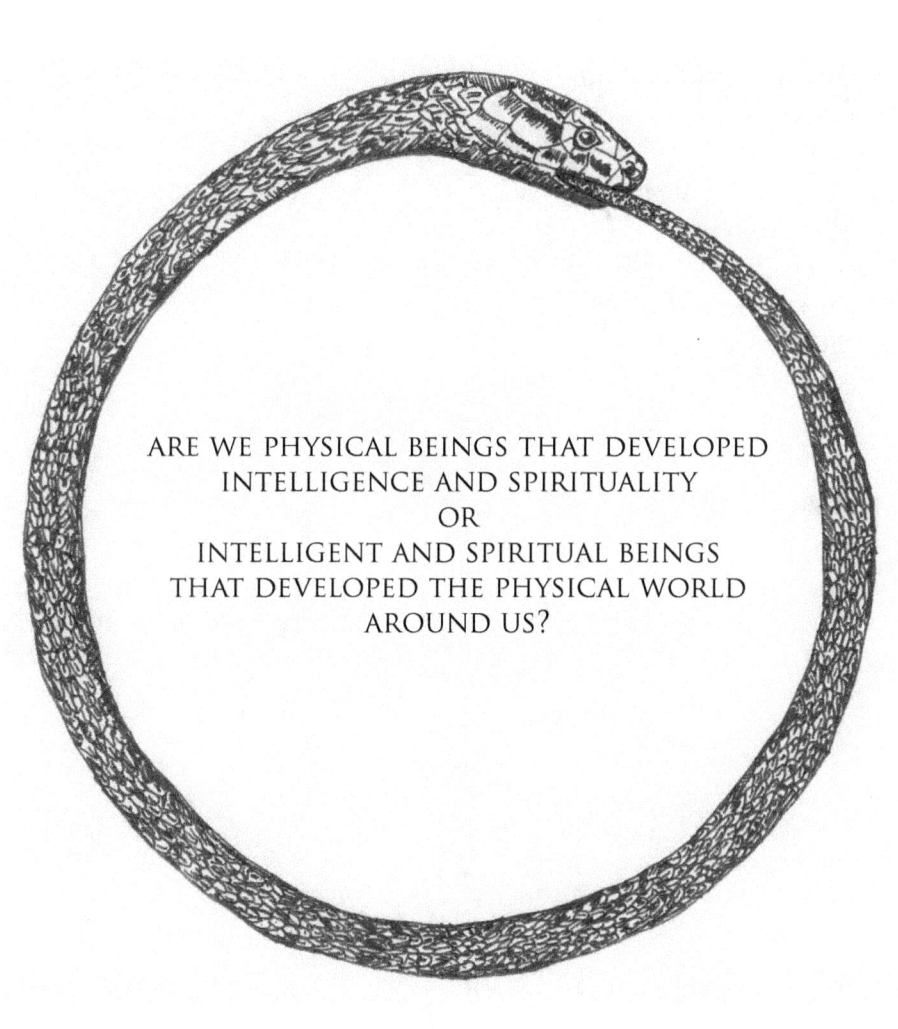

ARE WE PHYSICAL BEINGS THAT DEVELOPED
INTELLIGENCE AND SPIRITUALITY
OR
INTELLIGENT AND SPIRITUAL BEINGS
THAT DEVELOPED THE PHYSICAL WORLD
AROUND US?

**five more minutes**

it's in those
moments
between dreams and consciousness
laying in bed
drifting between both
that she procrastinates
over time
and presses the snooze button
to lie there
just a while longer
stroking the back of my head
the world reduced to
these moments
that give her fuel
to start the day

# love letter 22

Friday, May 2, 1993

Dear Roman,

Yo dog, what's snappin'? Sorry it took me so long to hit'chu back, but you know how that shit goes sometimes. Yo, that was some deep shit you wrote in your last letter. I wanna know what'chu been smokin, dog! I guess I never really thought about it all that much, but yeah you're right, they are puttin' an awful lot of hormones and steroids in food these days. This nigga here, shit, I'm use to momma's home cookin', but yeah, that does be makin' some sense why these young girls maturing faster these days. Shit, today between the Internet, fuckin' video games, movies and music, I think they mentally maturing too! See, I'm 'wit this fine honey right now, you haven't met her yet, but I rolled up on her like "...come n' get some of this R&B thug" and the shit's been like "Romeo and Juliet" ever since! Well... except I'm 20 years older, still fuckin' other bitches, and really I'm not as into her as she's into me. Hmm... I guess the only similarity is that her folks don't want me seein' the bitch, but if I start tossin' some money at them, I bet they change their tune real quick!! We be really conectin' n'shit a lot recently, and it's like we literally gots our own language now... baby talk! But gettin' back to what you had asked, yeah I think the age of consent should be lowered to thirteen as well. You gots my vote! But dig this nigga', I just read this book (and no I didn't just get out of county either, this nigga' reads in his spare time, dog!) that I want to turn you onto so that you can check it out, 'cause this shit was tight! It's an autobiography about a Polish-Jew nigga named Wladyslaw Szpilman who survived World War II. I know, right now you're like "...not another fuckin' Holocaust flick!", but dig this, this motherfucker, this Szpilman nigga' was a composer *and* a pianist... not unlike myself (hint). This cat avoided the concentration camps by hiding out in the Warsaw ghetto, which reminded me about the time I was hiding out in east-side Chicago on a warrant, but anyway, so as he be struggling to stay alive, music gave him strength. I think you know what I'm gettin' at by now... we need to "collabo" on this dime piece here! This shit could hit "all the right notes", ya dig? And my actin' skills are on point dog, so just throw a big fake Jew nose on a nigga' and the words are gonna speak for themselves!! We could be talkin' "Oscar" n'shit the way I've been feelin' about this piece. Shit, they might even grant your as a pardon if we hook this up 'cause you know there are tons of Jew sympathizers out there! Maybe then we can rip it up in my hood for a change, instead of me flyin' over there all the time. Have some bitches pissin' on us n'shit!! I know, I know... you have trouble peeing in front of guys sometimes, but this is different, they actually gonna piss on us, fool!! But anyway, hit me back when you gave the book a read and let's get on this shit quick!!

When there's grass in the field, play ball!!

R. Kelly

R. Kelly

* a letter from R. Kelly to Roman Polanski

A MAN
WHO HAD ERECTED
CURTAINS AROUND MOST OF HIS PERSONAL LIFE
AND PROTECTED THEM
PASSIONATELY
HE HADN'T ALLOWED ANYTHING
FUZZY OR TOUCHING
OR WARM
OR HUMAN
INTO IT
INTO THIS FRIGID PERSPECTIVE
NEVER-ENDING REPETITION
OF HIS
BARREN SOUL

THE FLAGRANT MISUSE OF
FORCEPS DURING MY BIRTH
HAS FOREVER DAMAGED MY
PSYCHE.

## the shuffle

as not to be defined
by the objects i own
i haven't washed my hair
haven't changed my underwear
in six days
and they're still kissing my ass
throwing rose petals at my feet
as i shuffle on by
against the grain
disheveled and high
it's all bullshit if you ask me

**hungover**

sunlight breaks venetian blinds
helicopters buzzing overhead
while morning trash is taken
spent taste of alcohol in my mouth
smell of smoke in my hair
and on my fingertips

                                            scratch   my
head
                                            scratch   my
balls
                                            scratch   my
ass
scratch another waster day
off this year's calendar
as i sit here in this discontent
clinging to some faded thing
that used to be
while last night's activities
cover the coffee table
beneath this clutter pulled my last smoke
cradling my lips
around its recess filter
why didn't the surgeon general
place a warning label on you
the sound of your voice
whenever heard on the phone
can you just come here
can i make love to you
i have other numbers
other women
but i don't want to use them
i might not leave the house today

## disposable commodity

I try not to come off like, feminist militia or some-
thing. I like men, don't get me wrong. But I like men
who are secure. I don't like men who treat women like
pieces of meat, you know? You're probably a nice guy,
and I'm not saying... Look, you're totally nice I bet.
And we're just talking, shooting the breeze, wast-
ing... you know, whatever. And it's not necessarily
that. But... Ok, this is what's fucked up with society.
What's fucked up is, that women not only can't just
fuck. Most of them. Some of them do. I tend to think
a lot of them fool themselves. I don't know. I can't
speak for every woman out there. But what I'm saying
is, there are these women that constantly obsess over
their looks. That are constantly judging themselves
against what the media's perception of beauty is. These
women think that the only thing they have to offer a
man is their body. And then there are some women who...
as far as the dating thing goes, who want... It's a lot
more meaningful, to me... I'm not going to speak for
anyone else, but I mean... When I meet somebody, I'd
just like to know that it was more about... me. The
real me. Do you know what I mean? I don't want to have
to worry if... I'll be around in a few months when a
newer model comes out or whatever. It just adds to this
fucking mentality today where men think of women as
nothing more than disposable commodities. How can men
realistically hold women up to standards that they
can't even hold themselves up to?

## public dis-course

you are free to watch television
billions of channels of mindless crap
which close down your sense
of infinity
billions of channels of mindless crap
which spoon feed you
illusions
of what you should
do
be
and think
the official explanation of events
designed
to ensure you see the world
in the desired fashion
react
in the desired way
messages not designed to inform
but to
direct and condition
but to
divide and rule
religious, political, scientific and economic manipulators
constantly position themselves between
truth
and the curious mind
speeding towards this Huxleyan world
Big Brother doesn't watch us by his choice
we watch him by ours

**she wore my kids well**

she was walking around half-naked
sucking
on a can of miller light
late that saturday afternoon
while i lay hung-over in the bed
what's your name again
she asked
fumbling with the question
and a pack of smokes
on the night stand
i changed the subject
to how amazing
our night was
or at least
what i could remember of it
and of those kisses
on the small of her back
that facial
and i'm not talking about the latest
mud-pack treatment
in beverly hills
we all long to find someone
who truly understands
or at least
will try
so while gathering my clothes
balled up on the carpet
she asked me to brunch
and i accepted
reaching into my pocket
and counting
the crumpled-up dollars and cents
left over from the night before
as her red monte carlo
sped down the avenues
in our town
i discovered the true beauty
within this stranger
and it was only while glancing over
that i noticed sunshine
reflected off the crusty dried semen
on the side of her neck
making me smile

**9x out of 10**

the better
a woman
looks
the more
problems
she has
that will break you
but
just put up
with that shit
and fuck them

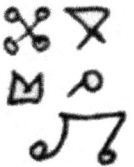

## sock drawer

i keep a blue metallic vibrator
in my sock drawer
underneath a pair of grey socks
and its use
usually depends
on how drunk i am
or how frigid
they are because
life moves by pretty fast
therefore i try not to immediately
wash it off afterwards
so that i can savor
their love
long after they've left me

REMEMBER THE FIRST TIME WE MET? I WILL NEVER
FORGET. RUNNING AROUND VEGAS, ROLLING,
THROWING UP AT LIGHT, AND THEN REFUSING TO HAVE
SEX WITH YOU ON MOLLY BECAUSE I WAS YOUNG AND
NAIVE AND I WAS CONVINCED THAT IT WOULD RUIN
MY SEX LIFE FOREVER. ALTHOUGH THE NEXT DAY WHEN
YOU ORDERED CRISTAL AND WHIPPED CREAM FROM
ROOM SERVICE JUST TO POUR ON MY PUSSY AND LICK
FROM MY TITS CHANGED MY MIND.

# star gazing

~~christine applegate~~ enjoys vanilla mocha blends, good books and sunshine at her favorite regionally franchised coffee house.

~~wesley snipes~~, ~~damon whitaker~~ and ~~halcum woodbine~~ like to smoke joints in hotel rooms with blonde, slightly overweight white women.

~~tara reid~~ and ~~andy dick~~ argue over the toxicity of bolivian-grade cocaine and apple martinis inside the bathroom of a pɹɐpuɐʇs lounge.

~~kirstan dunst~~ sometimes over-tips at the carwash when the attendant uses more armor all than necessary on the tires of her Mercedes SUV.

~~faye dunaway~~ is often referred to as a nazi bitch by the employees of Kinkos.

~~jamie foxx~~ always tries to drink your Cristal and party with your women when he's out on the town, but leaves before the check comes.

~~vince vaughn~~ will sometimes stop to sing "Sweet Home Alabama" with a street musician and tip the guy's dog a twenty just for keeping the beat.

~~edward burns~~ makes it a point to show up late to movie premier after-parties just so he can grab the giftbag and go home.

~~shawn wayans~~ likes to get the most bang for his buck when leaving a movie theater and stops to read each poster for the films that are "Coming Soon".

~~dave navarro~~ enjoys watching other men ask ~~carmen electra~~ for her number while working out inside the hyperbolic chamber of their local gym.

~~robert downey, jr.~~ takes his son to the grocery store for ice cream shopping sprees whenever he gets weekend custody or the munchies.

~~leonardo dicaprio~~ tries to keep it real and not attract attention to himself while sitting center court at NBA playoff games by simply wearing a hat.

~~justin timberlake~~ brings three extremely large black men with him whenever he goes out in Los Angeles because his publicist told him it would garner street cred.

## guarded

i'm easy to get with
go ask my ex
girlfriends
they'll tell ya
god's honest truth
didn't take much
to get me
twirling round and round
that finger
tap dancing on cue
once you get past
the walls
you'll wonder why they're even up

# *love letter 8*

December 18, 1984

Dear "Sweet Tits",

      Baby won't you please come home, daddy misses you. Now when you left me, you broke my heart. An eternal scented candle flame burns at the shrine consisting of a half-empty bottle of perfume, a bloody old tampon that I found in the trash, and several of your curly black pubic hairs found trapped in our bed sheets... call me romantic I guess? It began all so well... but what an end, what an end. When the blues overtake me, something about that scent in the air relaxes me, losing my urge to use your code and check your cell phone messages. Because all I have left now are memories, and they're even beginning to get harder and harder to jerk off to. "Chains of Love" as I so eloquently call it, otherwise known as "house arrest", has made me a prisoner in my own home. But I don't need to be telling my troubles to you, it was your signature on the restraining order wasn't it? This is probably just your feeble attempt to keep me from seeing other women. Keep me all to yourself, you "punky" bitch! But you know that I still love you baby, even though our relationship was nothing more than the sucking of every last orgasm from my body and dime from my pocket. Any more discussion of that would be treading in the past, an I'm trying to move on. I think you are too, or at least that's what it looked like from the bushes. See, my therapist told me I should begin to let go, and I have. Yes, I now have a therapist. And if by any chance you *do* run into him, I don't know, in court or something, please don't tell him about the shrine. He has told me several times to take it down, and might take it personal that I wasn't making much progress.

Sincerely Yours In Christ,

*Adolf Hitler*

Adolf Hitler

* a letter from Adolf Hitler to Soleil Moon Frye

## morning breath

everyone thinks they'e a poet
who am i to judge
women especially
i get it all the time
naked
sprawled out in bedsheets
while reaching for the roach
that was once a joint
they'll bombard me
with chosen words
from journals tucked away by time
so passionate in fact
the poem is usually followed
by the backstory of its
conception
i smile            i nod            i cough
from the hit
feed their ego
if not to just
get them back into my arms
to put the past away

**after party**

it's around 4am
when i usually begin to wonder
if these people around me are truly my friends

                it's around 4:15am
                when i usually get introspective
                analyzing these choices that i've made

it's around 4:30am
when i usually don't listen
then i crack a beer and snort another line

                it's around 4:45am
                when i'm usually out of cigarettes
                weakened by this substance coursing though my veins

it's around 5am
when i'm back to thinking nonsense
deliberating if everyone's just up to bring me down

                it's around 5:15am
                when i think i'm getting tired
                but really i've just had my fill of self-regret

it's around 5:30am
when i start making excuses
to myself and to everyone for the reason i must leave

                it's around 5:45am
                when i figure it's safe to drive
                and blend in with the morning traffic commute

it's around 6am
when i'm inside my car
questioning why i'm driving this fucked up

                it's around 6:15am
                when i finally get to my bedroom
                but now the sunshine's out and i cannot sleep

it's around 6:30am
when i try to beat my dick and can't
depressed that i've just wasted one more day

**cock**

i love my cock
women tell me that my cock is beautiful
i have a beautiful cock they say
my cock
ready to explode
when cradled by your gentle hand
thrusting up and down
manual manipulation
quickly turns into oral fixation
bend down and blow your brains out
shoot my load deep
exploding out the back of your head
blood, brains and semen splatter
the ceiling in some jackson pollack design
my cock throbs
the head
the shaft
the way it attaches to my balls
all beautiful
i love my cock
my cock is strong
sexy and dignified
my cock is insecure
scarred and naive
my cock, my cock, my cock
penetration deep inside your womb
my cock grips you like a firm handshake
but put my cock in your mouth
have a spiritual awakening
you will love my cock

## untitled

How is one to live a moral and compassionate existence
when one is fully aware of the horror inherent in life?
When one finds darkness not only in one's culture, but
within oneself. If there is a stage at which an individ-
ual life becomes truly adult, it must be when one grasps
the irony in life's unfolding. When one accepts responsi-
bility for a life lived in the midst of such a paradox.
One must live in the middle of contradiction, because if
all contradiction were eliminated at once, life would
collapse.

# STARFUCKER

you want to be the man
but still
you'll settle
to be the man
next to the man
next to the man
part of the entourage
so when boss man asks
what'chu think
you'll think
what he thinks
of course you will
because that's what he thought
why he asked
so that you can repeat back
his opinion
validate
his integrity
so you won't
miss the boat
or get a door
slammed on your foot

For many years of my life I've felt dirty. An impenetrable layer of filth has always existed upon my skin. No matter how long I bathed in the pools of regret, eventually it began to engulf my soul. Pointing the finger in blame would be too easy. Many do this nowadays, but not I. No, I choose this albatross around my neck. Somehow feeling it was part of a master plan. At the tender age of eleven, I felt his hands for the first time grip my small cock from behind. Calm words whispered reassurance into my ear, but something felt wrong. Naïve at the time and while under instruction, I unbuttoned then removed my pants and underwear. Forever burnt into my psyche is the image of his sullen gaze upon my hairless acorn-shaped cock. The receding grey hair, pockmarked faced man somewhere in his late fifties informed me of the normalcy of our actions. How this represented the purest form of love between a Father and his son. I believed this. I believed him. Only a few seconds passed before he dropped to his knees, engulfing my small ship of manhood in the oceans of his wet mouth. Only when ordered to grip his nipple while he performed this act upon me, did I even begin to become excited. Looking back, this act of inflicting pain upon my pleasure is a classic example of good versus evil. The harder I twisted his hairy pink nipple, the wetter his mouth became. I don't remember if I came that Sunday morning, but I do remember the footsteps in the hallway that brought his actions to a halt. Flustered, not being able to find my pants, I quickly put on my alter boy robe, then followed him to the door. Nothing was ever said, and somehow I knew never to talk of our actions. He put his arm around me and we walked down the aisle. Around the time that the cardinal wiped his lip while giving his sermon, I began to wonder... Could anyone in the congregation tell that I wasn't wearing pants while serving mass that day?

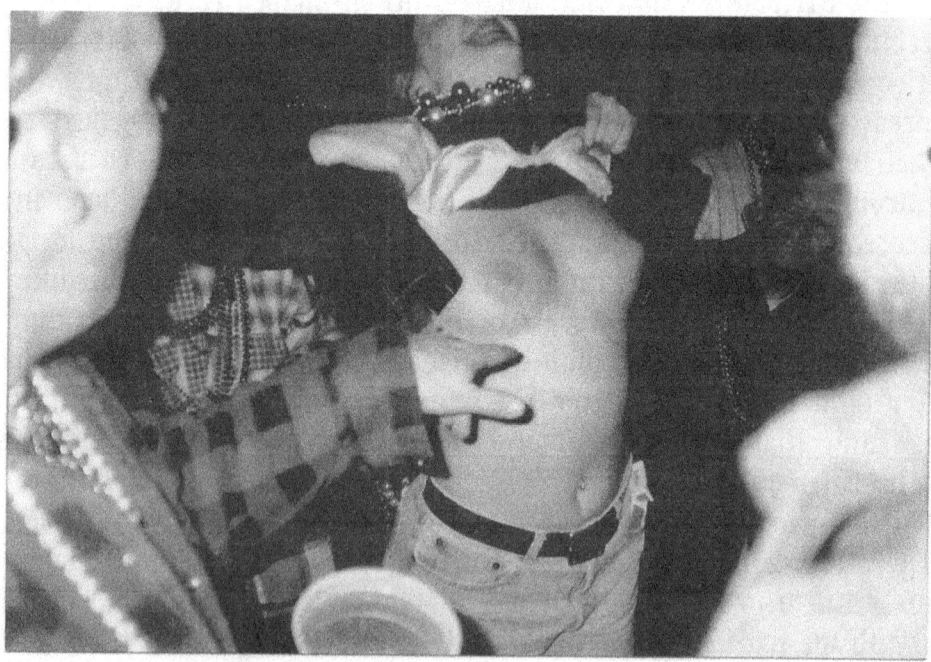

JULIA ROBERTS: I WAS THINKING... RED BULL SPEEDS UP YOUR METABOLISM, RIGHT?

SHIRLEY TEMPLE: YEAH, LIKE CIGARETTES DO.

JULIA ROBERTS: EXACTLY! SO I WAS THINKING....ME DRINKING VODKA & RED BULL AND SMOKING CIGARETTES IS EXACTLY THE SAME AS IF I WAS GOING TO THE GYM FOR 4HRS A DAY.

SHIRLEY TEMPLE: I WOULDN'T KNOW. I ONLY DRINK GINGER ALE WITH A SPLASH OF GRENADINE.

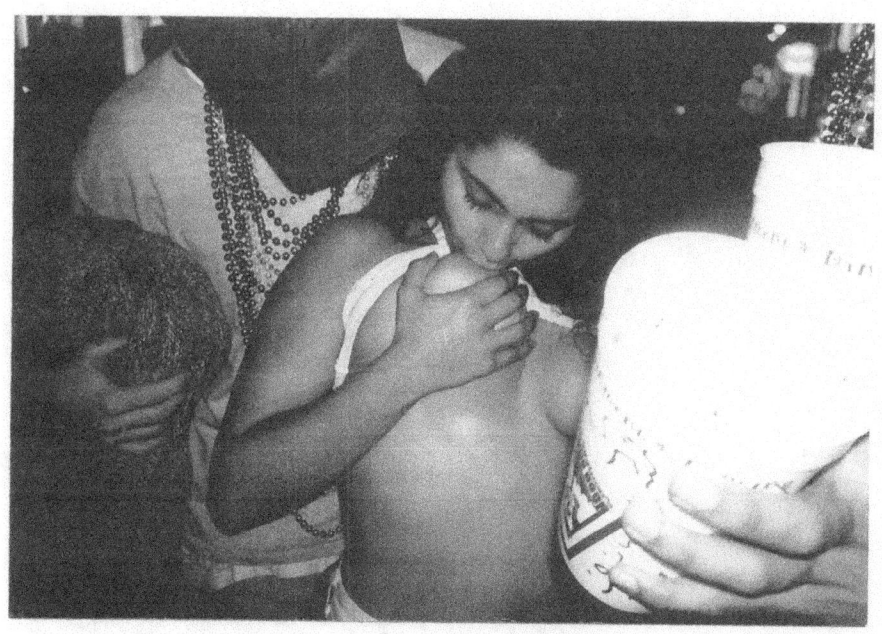

PAUL THOMAS ANDERSON: I JUMPED MY SKATEBOARD OUT A SECOND STORY WINDOW AND DIDN'T EVEN BREAK A LEG.

PHILLIP SEYMOUR HOFFMAN: DUDE, THAT'S AMAZING. I CAN DRINK ORANGE JUICE THROUGH A STRAW.

INT. HIGH-RISE BUILDING - ROOFTOP - SUNSET

Both with BODYGUARDS, The President of the United States
of America, GEORGE W. BUSH and the President of France,
JAQUES CHIRAC, look out upon the city in the middle of a
top secret meeting.

                    JAQUES CHIRAC
          I haven't got a lot to say
          George...

                    GEORGE W. BUSH
          We have time...

                    JAQUES CHIRAC
          I was kept pretty much in the
          dark. I didn't know all that much.

                    GEORGE W. BUSH
          What about now? Is there anything
          you could help me out with now?
          Anything you can tell me now?

                    JAQUES CHIRAC
          They got anthrax, that's all I can
          tell you.

GEORGE W. BUSH looks down upon his folded hands for a few
seconds. He then immediately rubs his temples while
looking out upon the city. With the silence, JAQUES
CHIRAC begins to backpedal.

                    JAQUES CHIRAC (CONT'D)
          ...I didn't know September 11th
          was going to be a hit, George. I
          swear to God I didn't know it was
          going to be a hit. Saddam Hussein
          bumped into me in Beverly Hills
          and he said that he wanted to
          talk. He said that you and Blair
          were on a big deal together... and
          that there was something in it for
          me if I could help him out. He
          said that you were being tough on
          the negotiations. But if they
          could get a little help... and
          close the deal fast, it's be good
          for the family.

                    GEORGE W. BUSH
          You believed that story? You
          believed that?

                                              (CONTINUED)

CONTINUED:

                  JAQUES CHIRAC
He said there was something in it
for me... on my own!

                  GEORGE W. BUSH
I've always taken care of you.

                  JAQUES CHIRAC
Taken care of me? You're like my
kid brother and you take care of
me? Did you ever think about that?
Did you ever once think about
that? Send France off to do this,
send France off to do that! Let
France take care of some Mickey
Mouse theme park somewhere. Send
France out to pick somebody up at
the airport! I'm like your big
brother George and I was stepped
over!

                  GEORGE W. BUSH
That's the way the Bilderberg
Group wanted it.

                  JAQUES CHIRAC
Well it ain't the way I wanted
it!! I can handle things, I'm
smart! Not like everybody says...
I'm dumb. I'm smart and I want
respect!

                  GEORGE W. BUSH
Is there anything you can tell me
about this Axis of Evil. Anything
more?

                  JAQUES CHIRAC
...the North Korean dictator, he
belongs to Bin Laden.

                  GEORGE W. BUSH
Jacques... you're nothing to me
now. You're not a brother, you're
not a friend. I don't want to know
you or what you do. I don't want
to see you at the United Nations.
I don't want you near the White
House. When you see the Statue of
Liberty, I want to know a day in
advance so I won't be there. You
understand?

(CONTINUED)

CONTINUED: (2)


GEORGE W. BUSH exits into an awaiting helicopter, while
JAQUES CHIRAC yells out to him.

                         JAQUES CHIRAC
          Georgie...

                                             FADE OUT:

**the complete man**

these are his needs:
the need for love and security ☐
the need for creative expression ☐
the need for recognition and self-esteem ☐

## prude

you probably take it missionary
every once-in-a-while
from behind
never swallowed
except when you're in love
which is rare
never had someone cum
on your face
or down the crack of your ass
never used a dildo
a vibrator
or a vegetable to get off
never had a three-way or a one-night stand
probably never had someone
eat your pussy
real good
male or female
never ejaculated
squirted
or gushed from sex
when you're not sure if you just came
or pissed the bed
you don't suck balls
toss salad
or give good head
get turned off by body odor
don't like to sweat
be sweat on
or mess up your hair during sex
probably won't kiss
right after he's gone down on you
afraid to taste your own juices
never role-played
don't like to be degraded
or turned on at all
when treated like a whore
probably detest the wet spot
make a big deal about where you sleep
and don't fuck on the rag either
never had your tits fucked
toes sucked

or a fist up inside you
don't like to be tied up or video taped
never got off on auto-asphyxiation
finger-fucking
your ass being smacked
or fucked
not comfortable with your body
in fact
you probably always do it with the lights out

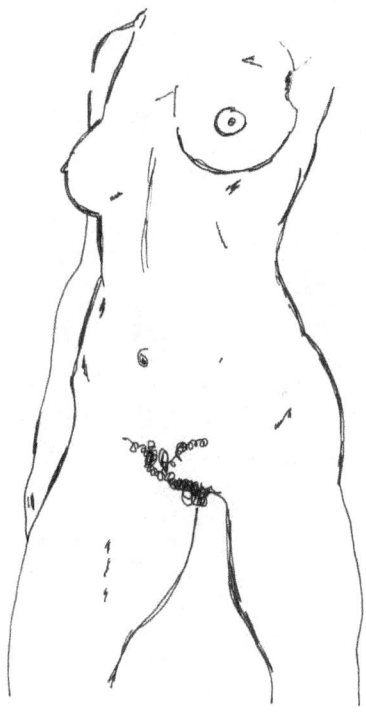

# CHAPTER TWENTY-ONE

The engine was running. While sunk in the driver's seat, Franklin waited patiently parked inside the hotel lot. This part never usually bothered him. It was pretty much always the same routine on Tuesdays. Not much to get worked up about on a day like today. He just had to wait in the car. Make sure that no one showed up unexpectedly outside the hotel room.

But something about this Tuesday was different. Franklin felt the heavy sense of urgency on his shoulders, which ironically lead him to sit up straight behind the wheel. He thought about the choices made that led him to such a life, then reached across and opened the glove box. A silver 9mm pearl handled gun sat inside, atop the vehicle's owner manual and a few unpaid parking tickets.

"Damn it Joey..." he said out loud, "This is the type of shit that will end up getting us pinched!"

Immediately Franklin closed the glove box and made a mental note to pay the parking tickets. He went right back to tapping his fingers in staccato precision across the top of the steering wheel. Then something caught his eye. Franklin took a few deep breaths.

He saw her walking back to her room wearing a yellow polka-dot bathing suit that complimented her golden skin tone. She was about 5'8, wore her hair short and was well-shaped. Dignified and sexy in the way his Elizabeth used to be. A real classy piece of ass.

As she passed by room 135, Franklin reached across, again opening up the glove box, exposing the gun. You could never be too sure in this line of work, and that's why Franklin was the best. He always kept his eyes open.

He was what you would call a "people watcher". But not because they interested him anthropologically. No, it was because all of his life, Franklin never felt truly accepted. By anyone in fact. Well, except for the only two people he had actually let into his life... Joey and Elizabeth. But it had been three weeks since she had left him, and he doubted her return. No matter how much dirty money Franklin continued to save away in the shoe box beneath his bed. Growing up on the other side of the tracks, Elizabeth was an uptown girl that had been around money all her life. It didn't impress her much. This he realized too late.

Once again, Franklin closed the glove box. He looked around the parking lot. Since nothing was out of the ordinary, he went back to the job at hand and focused on room 135. But out of the corner of his eye, he couldn't help but check out the dripping wet bathing suit as it walked away. He couldn't help but check out the onion-shaped ass that bulged out tight into those lycra bottoms. It was the onion-shaped ass that almost made Franklin cry, when it disappeared behind another parked car and into the hotel lobby.

Just then, the passenger-side door swung open. A man with a briefcase jumped inside then slammed the car door shut.

"Head this back across town." the man instructed, tossing the briefcase onto the back seat.

"Ok, but we need to talk about something first," said Franklin

"We can talk later, Franklin. First, you gotta get this package back across town. I got people waiting."

"No. We need to talk now." said Franklin. Slightly raising his voice.

Joey looked at his watch, then back at Franklin, then back to his watch again. Franklin pulled a pouch of tobacco from his jacket, rolled a cigarette, then looked at Franklin as he lit it.

"Okay," he said, "talk."

Franklin immediately sat up straight in the driver's seat again. He began to speak, but cut himself off before the first syllable had left his lips. This usually fooled people into thinking that he was slow or a bit dumb, but they were mistaken, gravely mistaken. Franklin had always been a fast thinker, but slow speaker. He enjoyed choosing his words wisely, something most people don't think to do much anymore.

Franklin then took a deep breath and glanced up into the rearview mirror. He thought about the best words to put this in. Being that they had known each other since they were seven years old, and being best friends for that long, Franklin couldn't bullshit Joey at all. But as with any friendship, even with all the good times they had shared, there were the bad times as well. The jealousies, the petty irritations that build up over the years. Inevitably it all has to come out.

"We go way back man," said Franklin.

Joey took a big hit on his cigarette, then pulled his cuff to check his watch again.

"Damn straight. You ain't just shittin' upstream. You're like my kid bother."

Franklin always hated when he said that. They were the same age. Actually, Franklin was four months older. A point to which Joey would always reply, "Age don't mean shit. It's all about maturity." This was solely based on the fact that Joey hit puberty first, and had fucked this twenty-two year old babysitter when he was nine.

"I'm done. I mean, after today, I'm done." said Franklin.

"Done?"

"Yeah, I want to take some time off. Take a vacation maybe. Get out of town."

Joey opened the ashtray. He slowly put out his cigarette then delivered a firm backhand across Franklin's right cheek.

"Your job is to drive my product. And being that you're the only person that I trust to do this. Being that we're partners. Being that we've known each other all these years... you're not done. You'll never be done until I say so. Trying to leave me high and dry."

Franklin rubbed his cheek. It still stung a bit. There had always been something sickening about Joey.

"Don't ever forget where I found you, Franklin. You were ghetto white-trash with a crackhead for a mother. Living on welfare. Eating out of dumpsters. It was my family that took you in. Remember that? Or do I have to smack some more sense into you? I made you the man you are today, Franklin. Don't ever fuckin' forget that. If it wasn't for me... Was I not the only one that was always looking out for you growing up? Don't I still? You want to go back to that? Fending for yourself? I thought we were a team?"

Franklin sat and thought about what he had said. It was true, Joey always had played the role of a big brother in his life. He was always looking out for Franklin growing up and still did. But as with most big brothers, Joey bullied Franklin. He tortured him. Joey felt that he was the only one who could constantly pick on Franklin. The minute someone else tried to, Joey would have their head on a silver platter. Because he also protected him, as most big brothers do.

"Do I have a first offense?" asked Joey.

"Huh?"

"Do I have a first offense?"

"No."

"And you don't have a first offense, right?"

"No I don't have a first offense Joey... and what the hell does that have to do with anything? What are you trying to get at?"

"Well, the way I see it. We're in business together until one of us catches a case. We'd be stupid to call it quits anytime before that. The way I look at it is... let's say we quit our criminal activity today. You have what, I'm thinkin', maybe a little over a hundred grand or so saved away in that little shoe box of yours, right?"

"It's none of your business what I have saved away," said Franklin.

"Come on Franklin. you're tighter than a Jew's asshole. I mean look at how you dress. It's obvious that you don't spend very much of your cut. But that's besides the point. What I'm saying, that if we stopped now... Big fuckin'whooptee-doo! You're sitting on a measly hundred grand. That's nothing in the scheme of things. You'd blow through it in about three years or so is my guess. Then what? You'll be right back working for the system. A nine-to-fiver."

"Well, the way I see it, nine-to-five is a lot better than five-to-ten no parole."

"They already have you brainwashed. Who's to say when you'd get pinched? You got a crystal ball I don't know about? You might as well hustle until you get pinched, no first offense and all. Maybe you do a year and a half tops. That's nothing. It could turn out to be tomorrow or it could be a few years from now when you're sitting on a couple million. Who's to say? You go, serve your time and when you get out, you never have to work again."

"Sure Joey, but I ain't comfortable doing no year and a fucking half."

"Franklin, you're crazy. Fed-time ain't shit. It's just like a stay at the Howard Johnson's. They got cable tv in the jail cells for christ-sake. Code of the street. You always hustle 'til you get pinched. Don't you realize nothin'? We're makin' these moves, right? Well, why don't we keep makin' them? Keep making that money. Who's to say we're gonna get pinched tomorrow or five years from now like I said."

"Yeah. I guess I see what you're saying. But it ain't for me."

"You guess? Man, that ain't no answer! Why are you

in the game?"

Franklin didn't answer. He just sat there with a blank stare on his face. But he was the first to notice the blue Ford pulling into the parking lot. Franklin also took notice of the driver, a young brunette with heavy make-up and fake breasts that stood out straight. She pulled into the parking space directly next to theirs. Joey reached into his jacket, again took out the pouch of tobacco, rolling another cigarette. Joey nodded to the girl in the car, then lit the cigarette.

"See, for me... I use to think that it was about the money.", said Joey, taking a quick drag then wiping the fallen ash off his pant leg. "The money that keeps me accustom to this lifestyle. Keeps me accustom to my trips to Vegas. Keeps me in these clothes and this jewelry. Keeps me able to afford the all-night partying. But then I realized... it's not the money that got me by the balls. I got plenty of money. No, it's not that. It's the hustle, man. It's what they call "the juice of the deal". It's like, why should I let this sucker go somewhere else to buy this product. I mean, if I can get what this sucker wants, why would I let him go somewhere else? I'm tellin' you, I can't. That's why I'll hustle 'till I get pinched. At what other job can I make five g's for five minutes work? So you understand how I just can't walk away from that. I'll stay making all the fucking moves I can possible make. Do my year and a half, and come out as rich as I can be."

Joey put the second cigarette, half-smoked, out in the ashtray. Afterwards he just sat and stared into Franklin's eyes for a few minutes, then shook his head in disbelief. Actually more disappointment than disbelief.

Franklin cleared his throat then said...

"I want..."

"You want what? You want me to score you some pussy? You want somebody's arms broken? You want someone's legs broken? You name it." replied Joey

"I just want out."

"There I can't help you."

The two longtime friends sat in silence for a few more minutes. Joey just looked out the window at the young woman that had parked next to them, then mouthed something to her. Franklin, feeling uncomfortable, looked into the ashtray. One last puff of cigarette smoke rose before the embers of tobacco extinguished. Joey pulled up on the door handle. Opened the passenger door. His alligator shoe stepped out onto the pavement.

"We set off down this path of crime. There's no turning back... Sorry I hit you." said Joey, before he slammed the passenger door shut. He walked around to the blue Ford. Once inside, Joey gave the young woman a big wet kiss and felt up her tits a little. Franklin just watched.

**criminal equation**

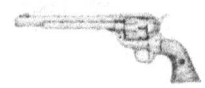

*curiosity + puberty + opportunity - guidance = voyeurism*

*rejection + depression x rage x lust - counseling - support = rape*

# *love letter 19*

Sept. 5th, 1997

Dear William,

Since I can't get you on the phone - How the heck are you... fine I hope. I just want to tell you I sold my house. I'm moving up to Kolkata with Sister Barbara. I will have 'till about the middle of May. I am so tired of living alone. I know you know Kolkata isn't too far away and you can come and visit. Barb and Fran would be so glad to see you.

I hope you are still doing good, if not, remember what it's like back in the Midwest! (Ha Ha) Pope John Paul II and the kids were over last Saturday, they were asking for you. Are you still dating that girl? She is very lucky if you are - tell her I said so.

Love you with all my heart,

*Agnes G. Bojayhiu*

Agnes Gonxha Bojayhiu

* a letter from Mother Teresa to Brad Pitt

**lesser of two evils**

the little boy came to the conclusion
that when no one is allowed to speak
words gain power
in a nation of twenty-five million
devoid of electricity
under trade restrictions
under totalitarian dictatorship
with propaganda posters plastered on the walls
manufacturing nuclear weapons of mass destruction
freedom of speech
just a foreign concept
in this environment
speaking out under such conditions
causes change
words can cause an uprising
revolution
a brand new day

**lesser of two evils**  [part 2]

the little boy came to the conclusion
that when everyone speaks at once
words lose power
in a nation of three-hundred and seventeen million
living high on the hog
under consumerism
under dictatorship disguised as democracy
with sensationalized twenty-four hour news plastered on televisions
manufacturing nuclear weapons of mass destruction
freedom of speech
the right of every derelict with an opinion
in this environment
kennedy conspiracies and killer bees
9/11 conspiracies and ufo's
words can be taken for granted
complacency
wasting the day

the little boy came to the conclusion
he must remain calm
find the best way of living in the meantime

## back in the saddle

But then... he left me. It's just. He didn't give me enough
respect and, um... he left. But I'm better. I'm better
without him. I happen to think that a woman doesn't
necessarily need a man all the time. That I'm kind of
working on that right now. Working on me. And it's kind of
a distraction because every time I'm in a relationship, I
end up getting the tunnel vision stuff. I guess I fall in
love easy. But who doesn't? You can just as easily fall
in love with a great pair of shoes as you can with some
guy that has nothing going on. And even if you decided,
right... Like, I'm just going to sleep with him and have
fun. I'm going to be a guy for once. Wear the pants. I've
done that. That's what I'm talking about. With this same
fucking guy. And I knew before I went on the first date with
him that I was not, you know... like, he was really not my
type. And I was like, "Okay, fine. I don't care. I'm not go-
ing to be fucking anything up. So I'll just go for it and
sleep with him." Well, I mean, I got along with him but,
I just knew that he didn't... He wasn't necessarily going
to enlighten me and we didn't see eye-to-eye on everything
and he was kind of blue collar in a sense. But he was also
very cool. So I thought, "Fine, I'll sleep with him". But
then it turned into this thing where we were friends and we
hung out and we'd sleep together. And then after a while,
he was just being an asshole and it was like, "We're just
friends". He wasn't getting possessive, that's the exact
thing. It's like... it was cool to just sleep together and
I ended up wanting more. Because I can't fool biology, you
know? I'm a woman and I can't. At the end of the day I have
to admit that there's going to be some kind of attachment.
Sometimes I think I'm afraid of love. I really don't know
what love is. I don't think a lot of people know what it
is. I think a lot of people just toss that word out there.
I love my friends and I love certain people, but what I'm
saying is... that in relationships, it's hard to tell
because there is a lot of manipulation. There's a lot of
this-and-that and I need something and necessity and lust
and love. It's hard to see clearly. I don't know. But my
dad left me before I was born, so that has a lot to do with
it. I guess I just want a guy to be there for me, you know?
I just want, like, to be in someone's arms. To be held at
night and told they're loved again. I mean, what's so hard
about that? I'm a nice girl. I have a lot to offer. Love
has its ups and its downs. I'm just sick of all the downs.
I'm ready for the up.

there will be nights when you want to give up.

when your dreams seem hopeless.

lost.

when living on pennies and balls of lint drive you insane.

but have faith.

**settle**

you feel like you don't know
what love is
except it's something watched
in movies
or read about
in magazines
you really can't pinpoint it
can't reference it
in your own life
but somewhere along the line
you've lost touch
built walls
gotten older
let people fade in-and-out of your life
without compassion
each time able to wipe the slate clean
you've given up
on idealistic fairytale endings
now you're just looking for someone
to roll over and hump in the morning
before work
to make it all at least
bearable

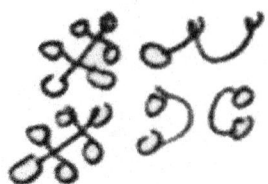

## forever faded in blue jeans

I think we had only dated a few weeks. And I'm not too sure why we went to the mall. Maybe to catch a matinee. Hell, I couldn't tell you. But what I can tell you is this. I'll always remember the gleam in her smile that brisk late-October afternoon. In a rush to dress I guess, she wore her favorite faded and frayed, broken-in blue jeans. They were the one constant it seemed in her ever changing wardrobe, since I was already familiar with them. I imagined the denim had been through a lot with her. So when she suggested while window shopping that a new pair of jeans was in order, understandably I was caught off guard. I'm the type of guy that doesn't mind shopping with a woman. In fact, I enjoy the experience. So anxiously I sat in the chair. The one outside the dressing room reserved for husbands and boyfriends, of which I was neither at the time. It was there I sat, with her purse on my lap, ready to observe poetry in motion. But after a few minutes passed and she stepped back out with the jeans in hand, I assumed they didn't fit. But on the way to the register, she explained it to me...

"Everyone has their favorite pair of jeans. You know, the pair. That fit just right. Are so comfortable that they just make you feel good. The jeans that have been through a lot with you. Because they're so comfortable, you want to wear them all the time. And you do. But after a while, you start to neglect them. Unintentionally at first, and they begin to stain or rip at the seams. Now you can try to wash out the stains or stitch them back up. And for a while they are almost like they once were. But with time, the stains will attract dirt again and even the strongest stitch won't hold forever. Everyone's constantly trying to hold onto the past and I don't know why. So today I've decided to buy these brand new jeans. I guess they don't have the same fit as the last pair. And are really not the same color. But I see potential in them."

Handing the jeans over to the cashier, she continued...

"See, today I realized that it's better in life to let some things go. Start fresh. I'm going to start fresh with these blue jeans right here. But this time I'll take better care of them and try not to make the same petty mistakes I made last time. Hopefully this pair will last a lifetime."

The cashier scanned the blue jeans, placing them into a bag. I'll always remember that gleam in her smile. Maybe it was the florescent tract-lighting, I don't know. But a warmness came over me as I offered to pay, and did. I took the bag and she took my arm as I handed back over her purse, as most boyfriends do. As we exited the store, I looked down to notice that in a rush that day or maybe out of habit, I had on my favorite faded and frayed, broken-in blue jeans.

"Come to think of it..." I said, "I could use some new jeans too."

What sick and demented creatures we are. Taboos of a puritan society long past have diluted into what some now call reality. We are puppets for a master. A master that convinces us, no matter how many strings they tie, we still retain our freedom. The master knows that the puppet's only wish is to become human, independent of these wires that control life. But independent thinking can lead to dark thought. At the car wash today, a pregnant woman sat down next to me as I waited for the undocumented hispanic to signal me that my car was finished. She was rather attractive to me. Probably in her early thirties, she had developed large breasts and childbearing hips. After several minutes passing judgement on my character in her head, she decided to engage in small talk with me. At first I was short with my replies, not being one to talk to strangers. The parental guidance I'd learned as a child would deem her unfit for me or the fetus, which I imagined she carried for her own selfishness. But at one point, out of pity for her, I found myself chatting right along about... What color she was going to paint the child's room? Had she already picked out the child's name? Was the slut completely sure that her husband was the father?

You know, typical mindless banter. The conversation never strayed from her. She showed no interest or cared to hear about anything regarding me. I almost didn't know it had happened, but I started to imagine... What if I held a knife to her throat? Would she beg for the life of her unborn child or would she pull me close, taking down my pants, in an eager attempt to suck me off for her own life?

## entropy

only now do you begin to understand me
decades past your decadent youth
a simple action
abstracted thought
of familiar scent will transport you back
like some distant melody
you'll remember me while stuck in traffic
from the roots of your soul
i'll drift back
hovering over your mind
endearing you
you'll wonder what it was about me
that has left such a vacancy
in your heart
you'll hunger for the touch of my lips
between your legs one last time
you'll covet our past
and with with blast of a horn
inch your car back into
the doldrum reality of existence
but when your take your foot from the break
don't forget to take the blame as well

## distorted images

When I was little, like three or four, my mother started
posting pictures of models from her fashion magazines all
over the walls in my room. She would tell me that these
were the beautiful women. The women who succeed in life.
She said they were perfect. The epitome of every man's
dreams. I guess I agreed. So ultimately I strove to be
that girl. That's how it started. Everyday we counted my
calories and watched everything I ate. Mother made preset
meals and constantly compared me to other girls my age.
Now this was from age three, to like, sixteen. She would
always tell me I wasn't good enough. I still had to work
on things. She was never satisfied. My mother had this
superficial belief of what the perfect daughter was and to
this day I am not that woman yet in her eyes.

# CHAPTER FOURTEEN

She was seven years younger than Franklin and in her prime. You know the type. That just knows she's hot. So she doesn't suck dick or take it in the ass. And if you do actually get the chance to get her into bed... after dropping a few hundred, she'll just lie there in the missionary position like a dead fish. But not because she's bored. No. It's because she doesn't know any better. She's inexperienced.

So as she walked by dressed in her summer clothes, Franklin quickly turned his head away and looked upon the setting sun. Shading his eyes, she mysteriously turned back around, approaching Franklin for a light.

He was about to be only the third person she'd slept with, she told him on their way back to his place in Franklin's 1968 Camero SS, the color of rotten eggs. He checked the rearview mirror and assumed that his two predecessors were probably high school boyfriends, then the thought quickly left his mind. But while drifting off he realized that they were also probably two-pump chumps, that never really, really got her off. Or cared to.

Franklin whipped the car into a screeching U-turn. He then began heading west on Sunset Boulevard. She immediately questioned this, but Franklin told her to just sit back, relax and trust him. After driving around in circles for awhile, Franklin parked the car on a side-street. He told her to wait in the car and that he'd be right back. Franklin left the keys in the ignition so she could listen to her favorite pop song. Which pleased her. He then exited the vehicle.

Franklin walked north, back up to Sunset Boulevard and directly into a fine Larry Flint proprietorship. He made some purchases, which totaled sixty-eight dollars and ninety-seven cents and let the cashier keep the change. He figured that he'd sixty-nine her. Only seemed fitting.

But by the time Franklin got back to the car, the smile on her face suggested that she had already figured out where he had been. Plus, the store logo being on the bag didn't help much either. Franklin popped the trunk, putting the bag inside, so that she couldn't check out the contents on the ride up the hill to his place.

The car ride home was completely silent. Not a word. She just stared at Franklin with a weird gaze of fear and excitement. Circling up into the hills above the boulevard, they finally parked and walked inside his home.

Upon entering, Franklin ordered her to go directly into his bedroom. Telling her that she should take off all her clothes and lay naked on the bed. Then call out for him when she was finished. She hurried down the hallway full of excitement and directly into the bedroom. Franklin sat down on the couch and checked his caller id.

She sang out for him when she was naked. Franklin was in the middle of rolling a joint. So he stopped, walked back into the bedroom and directly into his closet. He grabbed a silk paisley neck tie in haste. He always felt that solid colors were more seductive. At first she was reluctant to be blindfolded, but once again Franklin asked her to trust him and she gave in.

Once she was blindfolded, Franklin pulled a pair of handcuffs from beneath the mattress and cuffed her to the bed frame. This caught her off guard. He believed "you motherfucker" were the first words from her mouth, but couldn't remember much else of her rage because he had left and walked outside to the car. Opened the trunk.

When Franklin came back inside, she was going full throttle. Screaming out at the top of her lungs. Forcing him to run into the bedroom to quiet her down... because he has neighbors, you know?

At this point needless to say, she was a little pissed off. So Franklin went right at it. He removed the bottle of orgasm enhancement gel from the plastic bag, unscrewed the top, and placed a few drops on his left index finger. Franklin sat down on the bed, gently kissing her right titty which was slightly larger. He then began to run his finger, which was coated in the cool gel, across the lips of her moist pink pussy. Instantly, the yelling ceased. She just laid there. Naked. Handcuffed. Blindfolded and silent.

Franklin worked his fingers up-and-down against the underside of her clitoris. He passionately kissed her nipples while gently massaging her clit until the warming effect of the gel was achieved. She let out her first moan at this point, which immediately got his cock rock hard. He whispered into her ear that he would be "just a moment", and that he needed to get something from the kitchen.

She pleaded with Franklin to kiss her first. Which he sort of did. Teasing his tong around the outside of her mouth, but never fully kissing her. Franklin then readjusted her blindfold and left.

Once inside the kitchen, Franklin opened the freezer and removed two ice cubes. He walked over to the cabinet and took out a half empty bottle of chocolate syrup. Franklin tossed one of the ice cubes into his mouth, then went back into the bedroom. She was very eager at this point, and squirmed a bit as he sat down on the corner of the bed. She asked to be kissed again, which he refused. Franklin immediately began to finger-fuck her again, this time harder than before.

The precise moment she went wild, Franklin then dove down between her legs, licking her pussy up-and-down with the ice cube in his mouth, cooling off the effects of the increasingly warming orgasm gel. The metal of the handcuffs rattled against the bedpost as she began to push her pelvis hard against the ice cube between his teeth. Franklin could sense that she was getting a little too excited at this point, so he stopped. Walking back out into the living room, to finish rolling the joint he had started when they first got home. Being a pro at this, it didn't take Franklin but a second, but a clairvoyant moment consumed several minuted of his time. Drifting back, Franklin stood up, leaving the joint on the coffee table.

He returned back into the bedroom, immediately picking up the chocolate syrup and pouring it onto her perky little titties. At first Franklin was going to completely cover her body in chocolate, but realized that he had his good sheets on. Franklin didn't want to get them too messy, so instead he just made star designs on her body. Which he then licked off. While doing this, Franklin reached down into the plastic bag and pulled out the vibrator that he had purchased. He had about twelve already in his sock drawer, but always bought a new fresh one for the special dates. He was also kind of jonesin' to smoke that joint, so he went straight for the big guns. Going down on her with the vibrator and his mouth. Franklin placed the vibrator on the underside of his tongue, licking it hard against her swollen pink clit. She really got off on this and came instantly.

Her first orgasm squirted across the bridge of his nose. The second one, which tasted like warm honey, he managed to catch in his open mouth and quickly swallow. As she lay there shaking, Franklin figured it was as good of a time as any to go smoke that joint. Quietly he got up and went into the living room.

When Franklin sat down on the couch, he realized that he still had cum on his face. He took off his t-shirt and wiped it off. He lit the joint, enjoying his first inhale and her first back-to-back orgasm. He assumed about ten to fifteen minutes had passed when she started calling out for him. She said something like, "My wrists are getting sore from the handcuffs." Blah, blah, blah-fucking blah.

Franklin staggered back into the bedroom and lit a candle. Afterwards he just stood there quietly watching her. When the moment passed, he pulls her legs up into the air and spanked her for breaking their code of silence. She instantly apologized and asked once again for Franklin to kiss her.

Instead, he bit her nipple so hard that she almost cried. Franklin then ran his tongue back down between her legs and went at it again. This time pouring the chocolate syrup down south. Franklin loved the taste of wet pussy and chocolate syrup. It got his cock so incredibly hard.

At this point her thought about fucking her, but decided not to. Instead Franklin took the receipt out from inside the plastic bag. Then placed the plastic bag on his own head. For a short time Franklin attempted to suffocate himself, but then realized that the candle wax had already begun to melt into a pool at the base of the its wick.

Franklin removed the bag from his head, picked the candle up and tossed the hot wax onto her chest like you would toss a drink into someone's face. Sometimes Franklin just didn't think. Her chest immediately caved in, and for a few seconds, she held back a gut-wrenching moan of pleasure. The quickly exhaled, "I want you inside of me, now."

Very impressed with her stamina, Franklin lit a cigarette and stared at her for several minutes as she tossed-and-turned on the satin sheets. She was complaining a lot about the handcuffs still, which upset Franklin. He was about to undress when the telephone rang. As Franklin attempted to answer it, she pleaded

with him not to go. Turning back, Franklin put his ciga-
rette out of her hip for speaking out of turn. Then went
to answer the telephone. She let out a scream in unison
with the ring just before Franklin picked up.

"Hello?", answered Franklin.

"Who's this?" a muffled voice on the other end re-
plied.

"You called me buddy." Franklin responded in an ir-
ritated tone. "I'm in the middle of something over here,
you know?"

"I'm sorry." the muffled voice replied.

"Must have the wrong number, pal." Franklin was in
the middle of saying goodbye when the muffled voice
cut him off by saying...

"Love your brother. Respect your sister." Then imme-
diately hung-up.

Franklin thought it was a bit odd. He checked the
caller id but the number didn't register.

"Piece of shit!", he said. "Should just break down
and get a lousy cellular phone." As he picked the roach
out of the ashtray and put it into his glass bowl. Taking
a hit, Franklin drifted off into one of his "moments".

Drifting back, Franklin felt something wasn't right
and checked the time. When he realized that she had
been cuffed up for more than five hour, Franklin hur-
ried back into the bedroom. Somehow minutes earlier,
she managed to get her wrists through the handcuffs
and was sitting up smoking a cigarette on the bed.

"That shit hurt.", she said rubbing her thigh.

Franklin grabbed his car keys from the bedside table.
She was very disappointed when he told her to get
dressed. She questioned several times if she had done

something wrong.

"If it was about the handcuffs, I'll get back in.", she pleaded as she gathered her clothes and quickly dressed.

The whole time Franklin assured her that nothing was wrong, but wasn't very convincing. As he dropped her off back at the bus stop, she mumbled something about an intro-to-lit test that was coming up and that he should call her after she finished finals. Franklin noded yes, but in the back of his mind, knew that he'd never call.

Something had just clicked in his head. And for the next few nights Franklin couldn't seem to sleep.

REALITY GETS TWISTED WHEN LITTLE GIRLS GOSSIP.

## fickle

there she was
the first
beautiful woman
to lie in my bed
true beauty
from within
that she was
slightly
unaware of
eclipsed by twilight
while quietly running my fingers
through her coarsee hair
watching
refined elegance reflecting
off that little black dress
she fell asleep in
can't help wanting
to taste the night's wine
from her lips
wondering
if one kiss
could melt away vacillation
but this fantasy of perfection
can only dance in my dreams
frightened
that if she awoke from hers
things will never be as perfect
as they are now

SHE GAVE ME A MUJI
PACKED UP THE HOUSE ON WHEELS, HEADING TOWARDS EAST TEXAS
TELLING ME TO ONLY FILL IT WITH MY THOUGHTS OF HER
WHICH WASN'T TOO HARD
ALWAYS EASIER TO TELL YOUR FEELINGS TO THE PAGE
THAN IT IS TO THE PERSON

I WANT TO FUCK 12 WOMEN
AT ONCE
BE THEIR PERSONAL JESUS
JUST TO SEE
WHO WILL PLAY
JUDAS.

**casting couch**

welcome to hollywood
what's your dream
step off that bus and
into the sunset marquee
walk up to the bar and
get hit on by a famous
director
only in this town
can your life change over a drink
or a dick because
dreams are made      dreams are sold      and dreams are taken
so take my card
call me sometime
██████████
was supposed to meet me here for drinks
but ████████'s always late
worked with all the top names
in the industry
and i'd work with you
give you a shot
if you gave me head
act like you want me and
you'll act in my movies
there's the fast track and the slow track
star quality is something i can spot

## broken circles

prepare a feast
for my circle of friends draw near
be sure to offer them a drink
before setting the table
with grandma's finest linen
come
sit
surround me
let gallons of wine into blue plastic cups
continuously flow
like a marvin gaye melody
marijuana cigarettes pass side-by-side
with yesterday's news
let's get it on
seductively she sang into my ear
while we laughed like children
reminiscing over days gone by
gathered around the fireplace for warmth
these are not
the best of times
these are not
the worst of times
these are just the only times we've known
together
staring into the not-so-distant future
never aware
that life holds no promises
tomorrow
or the day thereafter
even the strongest circle can be broken
yet to thee we will always toast
gone
but not forgotten
i can't believe i'll never see her again

**charity**

i once knew a little girl
who had a single mom
that slept all day
in bed with me
until three in the afternoon
from being out all night
doing the hollywood shuffle
hardship i imagined
this little girl's life
was full of
at the pivotal age
thirteen
mom was twenty-nine
a pivotal position
she rode on my cock
right out of the pages of playboy
fame and money wasn't a problem
but for that little girl
i wanted more
and how uncomfortable
i would feel
each afternoon
leaving
while trying not to make eye contact
as she typed away
on her homework
at the kitchen table
probably thinking
i'm just another bum
that has taken her mother's attention
just another john
that takes more than he gives

**babe's and ricky's**

five dollars at the door
two drink minimum
here's a twenty, the girls are with me
"oh he's a gentleman, ladies..."
"watch after this one," black mama said
letting us take the big booth in the very back
then tucking the folded up bill into her bra
blues music and an open microphone
that's all this little girl needs because
on Crenshaw boulevard you can get your fix
scratch an itch or anything in-between
hers just happened to be music
old slim will take drink orders or clean tables for tips
but once that groove gets-a-going
he likes to dance
deep fried chicken, mashed potatoes, gravy and greens
bottled coronas and hand rolled smokes
this place has everything
watching her wipe the grease from her lips
on a napkin
she scribbled down lyrics that we might hide behind
dividing the simplest air into poetry
then a moment of clarity reveals she doesn't have
ambitions of Hollywood
still with mispronounced name
beauty took the stage that night
and immediately from my odd perspective
her lips, her hips, her musicianship
all began drawing me into the grip of
no ordinary woman
this girl's eyes spoke of fever and indifference
before a single note was played
"love me like a man," she sang
while secretly i wished
colored folk began swaying back-and-forth
clapping in rhythm to her beat
behind the mic
young, fair, and solitaire
her words forming gems so rare
as if to match those ruby red cowboy boots
in the end that night she gave everything
stepping off the stage naked
wrapping herself into a blanket of applause
i stepped outside the shooting gallery for a cigarette
her performance was like main-lining music
my arms now scarred where this girl's needles had searched for veins

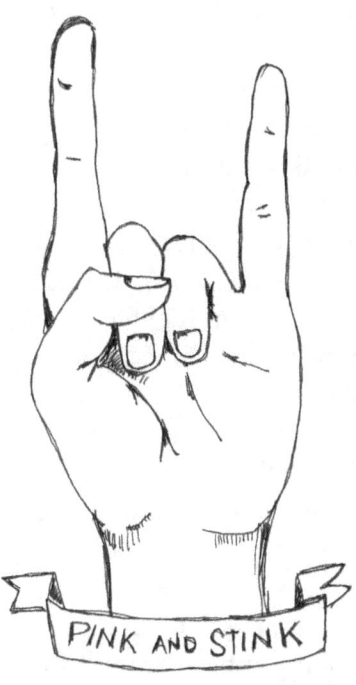

PINK AND STINK

I fucked an Asian girl last night. That little yellow lady was asking for it. Calling me up at two-thirty in the morning for a booty call. I didn't even know who it was when slant eye asked if she could spend the night. It took me a second, but then I realized that I had given charlie my number in an acid haze the previous Friday night. After giving the gook detailed directions, they are bad drivers you know, I thought about brushing my teeth but didn't. I figured that slopey might get the wrong impression and think I was looking for a relationship or something. It took all of five minutes and a shot of sake to get her to love me long time. I was curious to find out if an Asian honey pot actually split horizontally, getting tighter and tighter the wider she spread her legs. Upon further inspection while eating her sushi, which resembled a delicate flower wrapped in silk, I renounced the myth then laid into her like Hiroshima. Somewhere towards the end of out marathon session of sex, she mounted me, grinding away until beads of sweat and blood began to run down the shaft of my cock. I realized that behind her soft-spoken moan, she was actually chanting "round eye", trying to ride me to my demise like some twisted sexual variation of The Bataan Death March. I took offense to this and did not bother making her pancakes for breakfast the next morning before kicking her out.

**billy can't pray in school anymore**

my country tis of thee
sweet land of misery
that wants to murder me
because of thee i sing
therefore i de-pledge my allegiance
to these divided states of america
to this repugnant republic
of which i slam
one plantation
under fraud
unimprovable
with poverty and injustice for all
born into the land of disease
the home of the slave
my dick use to get hard
just looking at the stars and stripes
now i need viagra and a Hustler mag
larry flint for president
do it for the children

## and they call this dating?

from across the room in an instant i can tell
i can tell how far i'll get
your hair
your makeup
your style
all telltale signs
and that cosmopolitan you're holding
isn't helping much either
i've seen your kind before
a dime a dozen round these parts
just look around Marmont
you'll see at least three other variations
on that latest trend you're rocking
hip-huggers and gucci shades are out
so don't think you're different
because you're not
just sit there
try to look pretty
maybe some other guy not in on the game
will offer to buy you a drink
but not me
because we both already know
what would happen
if i brought you up into the the hills of xanadu
you'd suck my dick that very first night
pretending
that never usually happens
before shuffling to the door
putting your number in my cell
but i won't call
you'll tell your friends about me
but i won't call
and after a few days
you'll figure it out
then next weekend
someone else's dick will be in your mouth
and you want me to settle for that

### the hairdresser's cherry

After making the appointment. Showing up early. Flipping
though some back issues of Vogue.  Being shown to the
chair, then consulted about the style. Only then, when
the hair was being washed did he realize this: Getting
your hair cut by someone for the first time is like los-
ing your virginity. The two of you don't talk. Or if you
do, it's senseless patter. The process always seems to be
awkward, never turning out like you want it to. No matter
how many pictures you study. In the end, you both just
fake it, pretending to be satisfied with the job done.
It's only after several attempts that you both get the
hang of it, feel each other out, fully enjoy the experi-
ence then brag to your friends. It was around this time
that he felt the burn of shampoo in his eyes.

## tao of a madman

always fuck your friend's girlfriend's friends
but never fuck your friend
always write in pencil
but never write in pen
always fuck the bridesmaids
never fuck the bride
always keep your thoughts within
never let them go worldwide
always fuck your shampoo
but never fuck your soap
always bring the chronic
but never be the dope
always fuck protected
never fuck carefree
always try to be yourself
never think of being me
always fuck a Mary
but never fuck an Eve
always be the last one asked
but never be the first to leave
always fuck their lights out
never fuck too fast
always step up and buy the drinks
never flash your cash
always fuck her high and drunk
but never fuck her after coke
always share your cancer freely
but never bum a smoke
always fuck the boob tube
never fuck the book
always let them think you're shady
never let them think a crook
always fuck it juicy
but never fuck it sore
always play the pimp in life
but never play the whore
always fuck her personality
never fuck just her face
always wear gloves committing crimes
never leave a trace
always fuck with blackjack
but never fuck with dice
always get your money's worth
but never pay full price
always fuck like a perfect 10
never fuck like an alright 8
always write from sorrow lived
never write from thoughts of hate
always fuck the different ducks
but never fuck the swans
always give her just enough
but never lead her on
always fuck too early
never fuck too late
always binge with sinners
never dry out with saints

**they moonwalk amongst us**

Extraterrestrials landed in the 1950's. They will break it to us soon. Michael Jackson will be the perfect candidate. Now hear me out. He went from being black to being white. He spans all color. In third world countries they know Michael Jackson. They can't speak english, but they can sing right along with his songs. So he's loved by all nations. If you ever do get the rare chance of seeing him in public, it's like a fucking religious experience. People weeping. Falling to their knees and shit. So no matter who you are. No matter what difference you have. Race. Religion. Creed. Whatever. We all have Michael Jackson in common. With me so far? And I'm thinking Michael Jackson's message to us will sound something like, "I am one of many from another planet. We have been living amongst you for many years." Then he'll preach something about love, which by the way, all his songs are about in the first place. And dig this... Michael became friends with a kid that had brain cancer. The kid sleeps in his bed. Wham! Now the kid is perfectly fine. Michael Jackson cured him! So you can see how I'm definitely onto something here. He spans color. He spans religions. He spans nationalities. He heals terminal illness. He's an alien from another fucking planet. Mark my words. Come on, you connect the dots. There's something very fishy about it. Wait? He might even span sexes, because I've never seen him and Janet in the same place. Have you? Now if you start discussing his dance moves and the moonwalk, then you might be getting a little out of control. That's just crazy talk. You'd sound like a wacko because all I'm talking about is Michael Jackson being an alien. End of discussion.

10 - 16 - 00

Dear 'Noni,

What's up? I got your script. This one sounds real good and I like the title "Autumn in New York", it sounds pretty romantic. I hope everything goes right for you this time. If anyone deserves it, it's you princess! When do you think you will put everything in play? If you get that lead actor you were talking about you will be pretty much straight, don't you think? Did you show Matt a copy? I bet he liked it. Sorry about you not getting that "Marla Singer" role in "Fight Club", if you would just say the word that Bonham Carter bitch's legs could "accidentally" be broken.

So it sounds like you two got a nice place in the "Hills"! I can't wait to come out and check it out. Have you two been to any sporting events lately out there? Well things are going good. Like the song goes..."I have seen better days"! I am currently in the "hole" under investigation. They say they found some "contraband" in the common area. I never seen the stuff before in my life. I have been here a (1) week now. Hopefully I will be back on the compound by Nov. 1st.

I am dealing with it the best I can. I am locked down 23 hrs. a day. We shower Tues., Thurs., Sunday. They serve our food through the mail slot which SUCKS!! You and Matt both would be "anorexic" if you were in here. The only thing I eat in the hole is salads, chicken (1 time a week), the junk food, candy bars, crackers, chips etc... I do push-ups 3 times a week plus I read as much as possible and listen to the radio. Oh yeah!! SLEEP the most important. Probably 12 hours a day. Well before you know it this little vacation will be up. Then I will resume normal operations.

My softball team did real good this year. I played both A & B leagues. The A league picked me up halfway thru the season. We won the title in A league. In the B league we were runner up (2nd). We lost by one run, 17-16 in the championship. I hit the fence 3 times in the playoffs. Maybe next year it will go over. It is a 300 ft center field. Not bad for an old white guy!! How about those St. Louis Rams? They are still on fire. Minnesota also!! The Steelers are looking a little better at 3-3. My Cowboys suck. Aikman, it's time to retire and have some kids. Matt's two sleeper teams are looking good (NYG & OAK). I think the Raiders will go far this year. I like Tennessee and Denver out of the AFC & San Francisco out of the NFC. We shall see! Most likely it will be STL vs. TEN or DEN.

I should be getting in the program (rehab) sometime in Feb. or March. That would bring me home at the end of 2001. Hopefully before the Holidays. Well Miss Winona, that is about all for now. I hope everything works out with the movie and all. This could be the film that really boosts your career back into that "white hot" spotlight. But if not, you should try to pull off that pill-popping/shoplifting "publicity stunt" you're always babbling about! I swear it would work, and that's the kind of attention that will get people talking about you again for sure! But keep me posted either way. Tell the rest of "the crew" I said "what's up". I hope to see you in LA soon.

Take care,

*John Gotti*

John Joseph Gotti
REG. NO: 06353-068 S.H.U.
FEDERAL CORRECTIONAL INSTITUTION
BOX 1000   BATES UNIT
MORGANTOWN, WEST VIRGINIA 26507-1000

Ps. I heard Chris L. is home in one year, not bad. Also that fat piece of shit "Gabe" I hear is a rat! He should be home before me!

* a letter from John Gotti to Winona Ryder

# CHAPTER FOUR

Franklin rolled over in bed and checked the alarm clock. It was almost six o'clock in the evening. Soon Elizabeth would be home from work. If you could even call that work. She had it quite easy making ends meet, which upset him and led Franklin into the kitchen for a beer.

Liquid breakfast and a cigarette was his early evening routine. After finishing both, he walked back into the bedroom. Got back into bed, figuring that she should be home any minute if the traffic wasn't too heavy.

It was just after six when the shadows began to creep through the window into the bedroom. The seasons about to change, it was starting to get dark out a lot earlier. This was one of the many things that he blamed his depression on. His gloom. His hurt.

Having now been unemployed for a little over seven months, his writing was going nowhere. Nowhere fast. In the past they had all jumped at his submissions. Dozens of his short stories had been published in some of the top magazines of the day. He even came close to winning the Pulitzer once. Once.

But that was in the past and he was living in the present. And presently he was unemployed, being supported by her. While thinking about this, he pressed a pillow over his face in a feeble attempt to suffocate himself. This too was part of his daily routine.

It was around six-thirty when he heard her keys fumbling at the front door. He removed the pillow from his face and adjusted his hair. Ran his right hand across his chest then down into his underpants and scratched. Brought his hand back up and under his nose. Took a big whiff and decided that even though he hadn't showered in three days, he still smelt good. Manly. That was important to him.

By this time he could already hear her in the living room shuffling through the mail. He assumed they were probably all bills. Electric bills. Gas bills. Water bills. Credit card bills. That's why he never got the mail anymore. He couldn't afford to.

It was shortly after when he heard the footsteps echoing down the hallway. Then the bedroom door opened.

"Mmmm... I've been dying to suck your cock all day." she immediately said upon entering.

He just laid there. Pretending to be asleep. She slowly began to unbutton her silk blouse. Gotten all the way down to the fourth button, before he peeked and noticed she wasn't wearing a bra that day. She had great tits and knew it. Gay guys always wanted to grope them. See if they were real, and they were.

After removing the blouse, she ran both hands back-and-forth against her chest. Gripping those firm titties in both palms, then slowly moving one hand down underneath her skirt.

"I want your cum on my face. I'm thirsty. Baby, pull down your underpants and let me have some of that cock. Give it to me. Baby? Wake up." she screamed.

He rolled over onto his side, turning his back to her. Still pretending to be asleep. She walked over and sat down next to him on the bed. Bending over she whispered into his ear. "Baby come on, give me some of that hard juicy cock. Some of that nice, long, thick cock. Mmmm... I'm so fucking horny. Oh baby, please. I need some cock. Feed me some of that hot, sweet cum. Give me some now." she purred into his ear while grinding both of her hands under her skirt now.

He turned towards her and looked deep into those green eyes. Right on cue, she went directly down on him. Taking the whole thing into her mouth at once. He leaned his head back and closed his eyes. Just then, her lips came off from around his dick. He opened his eyes and looked back down at her. She spit on it and began to jerk him off.

"God, my pussy's wet for you." she said, running her tongue up-and-down against the shaft of his cock.

He just laid there.

Every once-in-awhile, he'd look down at her performance. But mostly he just kept his head back and his eyes shut. She took his dick from her mouth and began to work it again with her hand. Up-and-down. Up-and-down. Faster and faster. The whole time moaning.

"I love your cock in my mouth. Baby, I'm so cock hungry. I'm a cock hungry bitch!" Then went right back down on him, trying to suck the life from his already weakened body. "I'm so wet. Baby, jam me down my throat. Shoot a load down my throat. I want to taste your cum."

His hands gripped the bed sheets. She was sucking and touching and moaning even more than before. She sucked away, then ran her tongue down towards his balls. Which she also took into her mouth. His firm grip finally pulled the bed sheets from the corners of the bed. He was about to cum.

She felt his balls tightening in her mouth, and quickly wrapped her mouth again around the head of his dick. As not to miss a drop. Again he looked deep into her green eyes. Ran his fingers through her long blonde hair. She always knew that he was seconds away from orgasm when she felt the firm grip of her hair. She closed her eyes and began to swallow every last drop. He just laid there shaking a bit, when she finished.

"Mmmm... I love your cock. Thank you for saving me your cum. Oh thank you baby," she said wiping the corners of her mouth clean.

When she was asking if he had gotten any work done that day, he pulled a cigarette from the night stand and lit it.

"Baby, a writer needs to write," she said. "You need to quit being so hard on yourself, on your work and just write. Write about the first thing that inspires you. Anything. Just to try to get something down on the page."

He smacked her across the face and told her to get dinner on the table. With a tear in her eye and cum on her breath, she left to the confines of the kitchen.

She had no clue what it meant to be a great writer. Just write something? That was absurd. Who would want to read something he "just wrote"? No one. People want to read about love, about pain, about resurrection, about... then it dawned on him.

While she was busy boiling spaghetti in the kitchen, he got up out of the bed and walked over to the corner of the room. Pulling the old typewriter from underneath some dirty clothes in the closet. He checked the ribbon. It was still in pretty good shape. He fed a piece of paper through and instantly began to type:

"He rolled over in bed. Checked the alarm clock. It was almost six o'clock. Soon she would be home from work."

He banged away at the typewriter for the next three nights. It felt good. It was she who had found the remedy.

IF YOU DON'T RAISE ME UP
TO HEAVEN,
I WILL CAST YOU DOWN TO
HELL.

FOR ME,
A WOMAN MUST BE:
LOVING,
ADORING
AND FORGIVING.

ㅈꝑꝰꝥE

models settle down fast because of their lifestyle.
they're always traveling in different countries. making
friends and leaving again. that when they meet a guy,
they just want to chill. get comfortable. it's a lonely
life traveling by yourself.

I'VE BEEN DEGRADED FROM GIRLFRIEND....

TO LOVER ... .

TO BOOTYCALL.....

BUT I'LL NEVER BE YOUR BITCH!

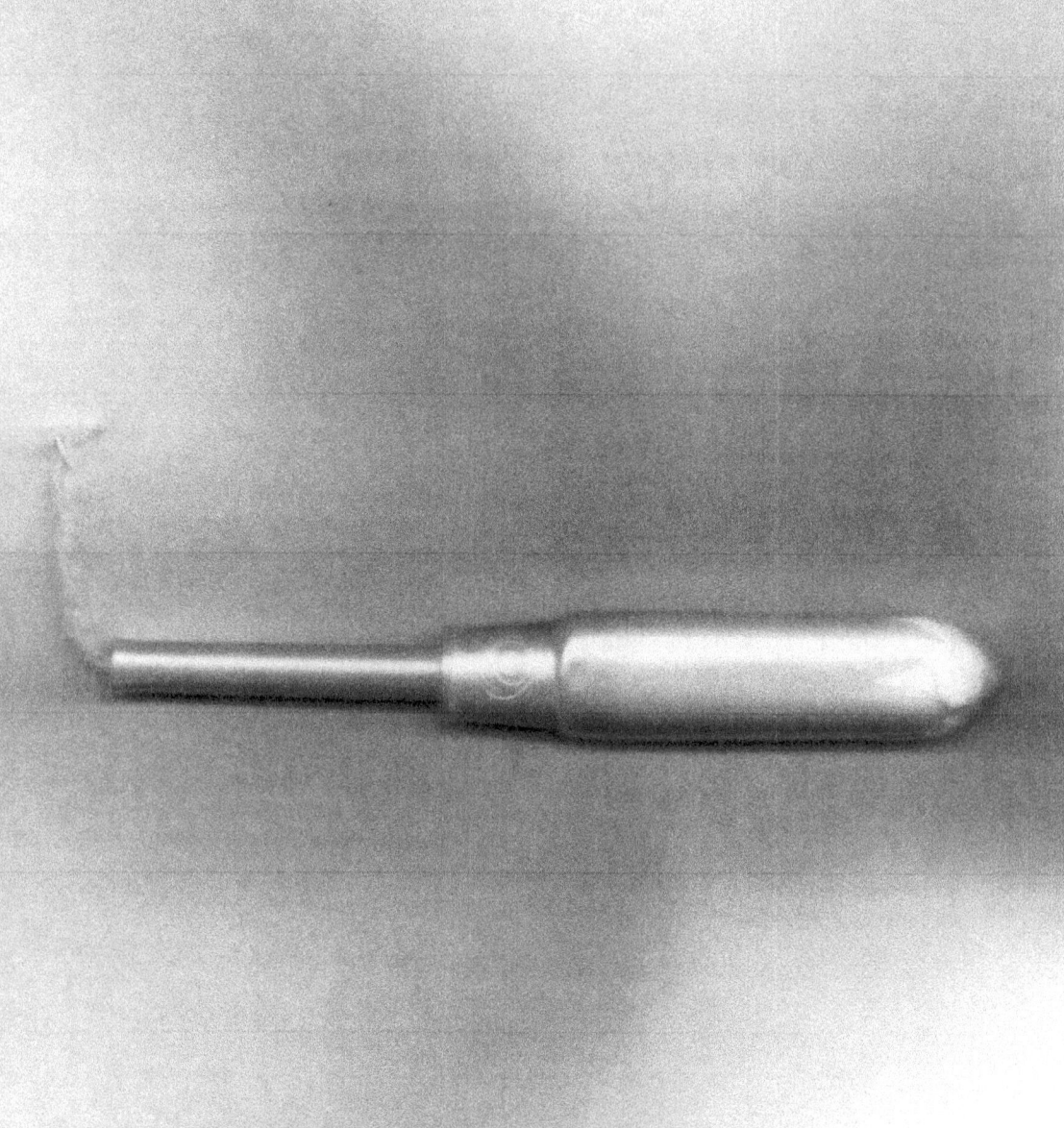

WHENEVER I SEE TAMPON COMMERCIALS
WITH COUPLES, I ALWAYS FEEL SORRY FOR
THE ACTOR PLAYING THE BOYFRIEND....
BECAUSE WE ALL KNOW HE'S NOT GETTING
ANY UNLESS THE ACTRESS IS A DIRTY SLUT.

### different breed of evil

Only as I sat covered in blood, did I release the polaroid pictures from my grip and began to retrace the steps that lead me into her closet in the first place. I guess she was around my fourth, or maybe my fifth. I'm not sure. But generally you can stalk and kill human prey in one of three ways: the nomadic, the territorial or the stationary methods. Each has their merit. Pros and cons, if you will. And you usually stick with the one that brought you to the death dance. But no matter what, particularly when in risk of capture, there always comes time to change his or her technique. So I sought to discover a new method of release, who could blame me? At first because of the randomness of my anger, my executions were swift. But this time she actually invited me inside her home, to which I wasn't accustom. I guess she had enjoyed the evening we shared, or was lonely because of her recent breakup. I'll never know. But since I had all the time in the world, I slit Susan from her throat to her groin, disemboweled, then wore her like a jacket. Susan was a tight fit, but I managed. Prancing around the room as if the jacket were a Christmas present I had always wanted as a child. But wait. I'm jumping ahead. You probably wanted details, right? Alone inside Susan's home I had time for every deviant, lustful desire I could imagine and believe me I took full advantage. But I'm not one to kiss and tell. Let's just say she had a throat like velvet and a pay-per-view pussy and leave it at that. I always make sure not to leave any forensic evidence. Something picked up from my many hours spent watching the Discovery Channel and the CSI franchise, so wiping the crime scene clean of finger prints and DNA is a must. In what other little spare time I have, I enjoy the conceptual arts. So I think it was around the time I was scattering her intestines across the floor or looking around her home for some rope or extension cord to bind Susan' lifeless body to the wall with that I stumbled across the shoe box of old pictures and love letters. Only looking back upon the life she had once lived, did I regret removing her womb. The defining feature of womanhood I came to despise, and eating it. I think that many wrestle with the same demons as I, but most are able to defeat these thoughts. Only a few, myself included, are able to act upon them. This savage crime will only reveal my most dreaded, macabre, inhuman fascination with evil. One day men will look back and say that I gave birth to a new millennium.

INT. HIGH-RISE BUILDING - WORKOUT ROOM - EVENING

Two muscular, toned men in their early thirties sit
inside the sauna.

                    FRANK
          I'm so glad that I finally got to
          meet you. I've seen you around the
          building before, but never put the
          face and the name together. I've
          heard so much about you.

                    DUNCAN
          Likewise. I'm happy to finally
          meet you because now we finally
          have another couple to go out with
          on the weekends. We all should go
          to dinner sometime, you know?

                    FRANK
          That would be nice. We should
          definitely do that. I know this
          great sushi bar in Malibu.

                    DUNCAN
          Amazing!

                    FRANK
          But we'll have to do it soon
          because we are going to be moving.

                    DUNCAN
          Moving?

                    FRANK
          Yes. We are moving in a few weeks
          to Maui. I have a job offer there.

                    DUNCAN
          You know, I think I did hear that.
          I love Maui! We got married there.
          You have to make it to Sunset
          Beach, it is so beautiful there.

                    FRANK
          Oh my god, we got engaged there!
          Yes, I love Maui. I'm more of a
          sunny, dry weather person, so I'll
          fit right in.

                    DUNCAN
          You're really lucky to have a
          partner like Bob. He's such a
          great guy.

                                        (CONTINUED)

CONTINUED:

                    FRANK
          Thanks. Yes, he is... And my
          parents just love him! That's the
          important part. I remember the
          first time I brought Bob home. I
          guess the glow I gave off, my mom
          could just tell how happy I was.
          She said she had never seen me so
          happy before.

                    DUNCAN
          Aww, that's sweet.

                    FRANK
          Thanks... And my father, he gave
          Bob this great big hug and a kiss
          on the cheek and said... "Take
          care of my boy."

                    DUNCAN
          Yes, Fred's parents are great as
          well. He has four older brothers
          and it's a staple on Christmas
          that his mom buys them all socks
          and underwear. Well, last
          Christmas when we visited and I
          opened my gift... Bam! Socks and
          undies! It made me feel so good.
          Acceptance, you know? I feel like
          I'm the fifth son.

                    FRANK
          That is so touching, I have a
          feeling that when we move to Maui,
          we'll be seeing the two of you a
          little more than we do now.

The two sweaty men stand up to exit. While stopping at
the door to embrace, DUNCAN's towel falls to the ground.
FRANK quickly bends down to pick it up and begins giving
DUNCAN a blowjob.

## public enemy number one

call the white house
call the governor
they're aware of my problems
monitor my brain waves
pagans, blacks, abortionists, jews
lesbians, muslims, mexicans and gays
i hate to throw ice on everyone's erections
but it's me
who is being persecuted
by the powers that be
and not because of my sex, race, religion or
creed
the simple prejudices
that consume humanity
i'm on another level
and proud to be on every nation's
most wanted list
because of knowledge
passed down to me
from outer space
which i'd be willing to share
but only if
you agree to pass it on as well
i know and have always known
that the earth
is a global Alcatraz
a spinning ball
of control and restraint
dictated by the few
at the expense of the many
**New World Order**
is just around the corner
but only because
we have developed idle minds
ok, ok, i know what you're going to say
it's incredibly difficult
for a relative small
handful of people
to control the lives of nearly
seven billion strong

but it's comparatively easy
once you have control of education
and the media
once you control the messages that bombard
the conscious and subconscious mind
from cradle to grave
once you have conditioned one generation
to think the way you require
it becomes even easier to condition the next
programmed parents
now unknowingly working on your behalf
sadly society blindly
accepts
so much that is passed down
and there is no virtue in being blind when you have eyes
the vast herds of humanity are living a lie
denying what they really believe
denying what they want to do with their lives
stop denying yourself
stop living that lie
join me
i have written numerous threatening letters to
the united nations
and i encourage you to do the same
make sure to reference this diversion
used to manipulate us
democracy
is not
freedom
do not be mistaken
democracy
is not another word for
freedom
as you've been led to believe
51 people telling the other 49 what to do
is not
independence

SAY WHAT YOU WISH
CALL ME INSANE
BUT IT'S FAR BETTER TO WALK
THAN TO RUN IN THE RAIN

## v.i.p.

everybody
always knows somebody
that can get you in
because this is the place to be
and be seen
expensive drinks
valet
eye candy
you get what you pay for
and it's all on display
in this fairy tale world
everyone's a rockstar
so go-ahead
brag to your friends
about all the pseudo-celebrities you saw
behind the velvet rope

I ATE TWO BURGERS. HE DARED ME TO EAT TWO MORE, BUT I DIDN'T WANT TO. I WAS PAST HAVING TO LOOK BACK ON THAT NIGHT, OR BEING KNOWN AS THE GUY THAT ATE FOUR CHATEAU MARMONT BURGERS WITH FRIES.... BUT I COULD HAVE.

**family crest**

all you're given was his name
his name and his pain
pain, disturbing pain
flowing through your veins
the toxic combination of venom and blood
fatal to most
has driven others to infamous heights
that hate you're feeling
is a fucked up thing
said the bastard black sheep son
stepping out into the light
but when cooked up and mainlined properly
stardom rises like the empty syringe
and if you chase this dragon
then they'll chase you
he whispered before vanishing back
into the darkness
they'll yearn to taste your soul
lick it clean
ask for seconds
this quest for love
will only drench you with indifference
sure poppa was a rolling stone
who cares if he kissed you goodbye
harnessing hatred is what got you up and rolling
however this movement
will soon be for not
troubled mockery calls out from the shadows
you can be adorned by many
but it is still he
who will never call

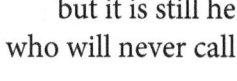

**super skank**

you've spent a lot of time
at tanning booths
trying to perfect that unnatural orange
cancer-ridden alligator glow
spent a lot of time
in the bathroom at your gym
working on your abs
bent over the toilet bowl
jamming your middle finger down your throat
throwing up salads and cigarettes
spent a lot of time
at the cosmetic surgeon
bleaching your soy latte stained teeth
thinking botox and silicone will finally define you
f-a-k-e  a-s-s  b-i-t-c-h
you've spent a lot of time
in boutiques, department stores, strip malls and vintage stores
shopping for plastic clothes
charging money you don't have on trendy shoes
constantly trying to disguise yourself
or show skin for social acceptance
sticking shit up your nose
thinking life's a party
hanging at bars
getting that v.i.p treatment
snorting fairy dust won't turn cinderella into a princess
f-a-k-e  a-s-s  b-i-t-c-h
you've spent just as much time
constantly talking and running off at the mouth
especially on your cell phone
it's always the same thing
me, me, me
off chance it's not
typical he-said-she-said-shit consumes your time
caught up in gossip
other people's problems
other people's lives
with your fake hair, fake nails, and fake tits
is anything about you real
basically you've just spent a lot of time running
to the salons, to the gyms, to the malls, to the bars, to the drugs

thinking it's solely your
physical shortcomings
that have held you back all these years
so far you've spent your whole life running
mostly from yourself

SHE WAS VIOLATING MY STANDARDS
FASTER THAN I COULD LOWER THEM.

MAKING OUT WITH A PREGNANT CHICK IS
LIKE HAVING A THREE-SUM.

I OPEN MOUTH KISSED A WHORE,

TASTED THE LAST JOHN'S SEMEN.

WANTED TO SEE IF SHE REALLY LIKED ME, THE REAL ME,

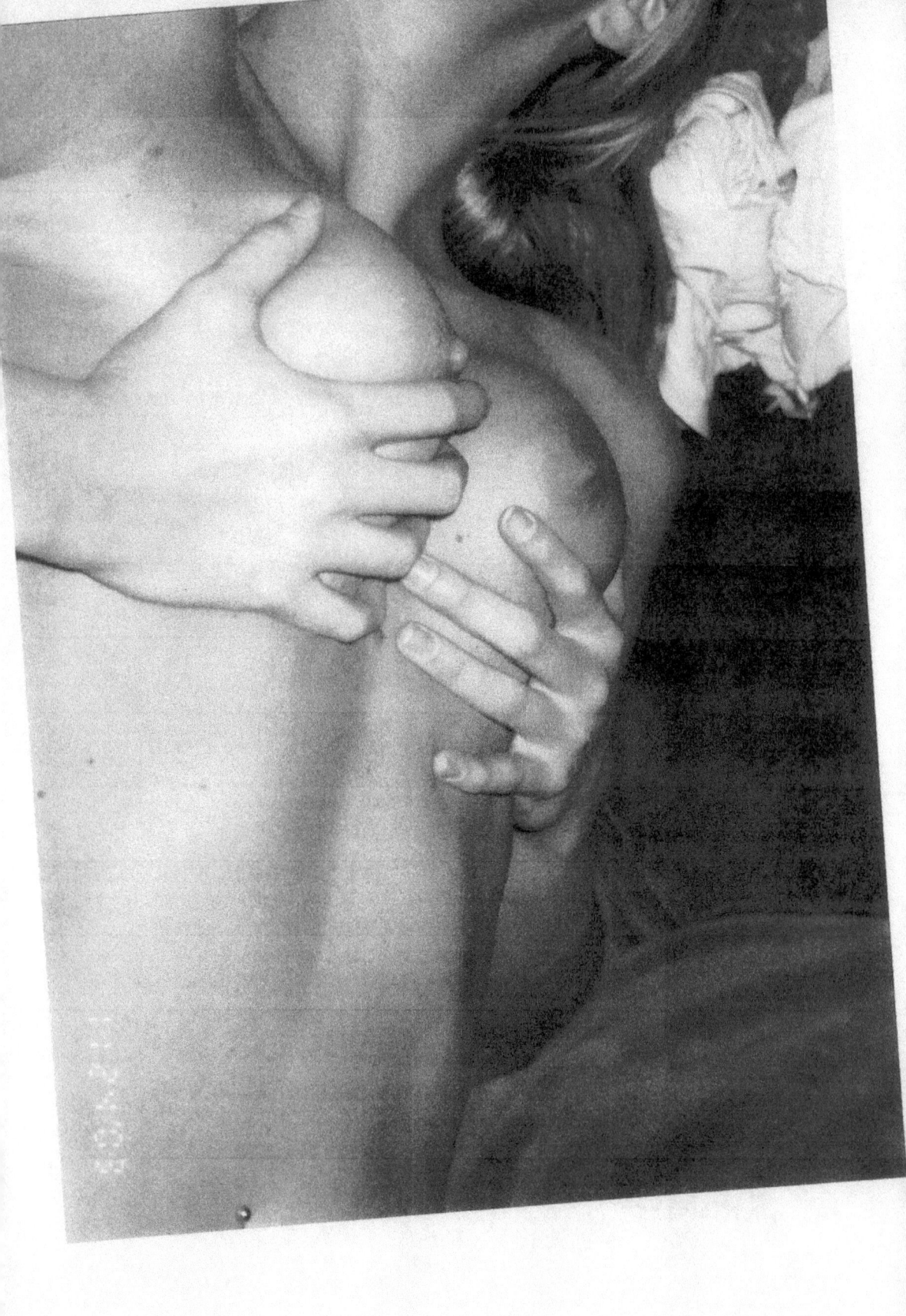

## a wounded heart

anyone can fuck
but no future lover
would ever match
his determination
but incapable
of love
he looked deep into her eyes
hoping she'd soon forget
everything that he'd shared
be it the wetness
of his kiss
upon her lips
or his fingertips
brushing across her tits
or between her legs
how time
seemed so unimportant to her
when lying in his embrace
for countless afternoons
swapping certain responsibilities
for his unpredictable love
the worshiping of the slit
between her legs
as if it were a golden calf
he looked deep into her eyes
for one last time
but she was nowhere to be found

The End

www.ingramcontent.com/pod-product-compliance
Lightning Source LLC
Chambersburg PA
CBHW080829250626
47160CB00008B/2886